M000043302

THE BRIEFCASE

ROBERT NESTOR MAKI

Copyright © 2000 by Robert Nestor Maki.

Library of Congress Number: 00-191273

ISBN #: Softcover 0-7388-2495-X

All rights reserved. No part of this book may be reproduced or transmitted in any form or by any means, electronic or mechanical, including photocopying, recording, or by any information storage and retrieval system, without permission in writing from the copyright owner.

This is a work of fiction. Names, characters, places and incidents either are the product of the author's imagination or are used fictitiously, and any resemblance to any actual persons, living or dead, events, or locales is entirely coincidental.

This book was printed in the United States of America.

To order additional copies of this book, contact:
Xlibris Corporation
1-888-7-XLIBRIS
www.Xlibris.com
Orders@Xlibris.com

BEALS MEMORIAL LIBRARY
50 Pleasant Street
Winchendon, Mass. 01475
tel. 297-0300

THE BRIEFCASE

CONTENTS

This novel is dedicated to my first love,
Clare, my wife of 23 years
and mother of our two children, Kristin and Eric.
Her love and dedication to family gave my life new meaning
and her courage will remain a beacon in my life.

CHAPTER ONE

Not a typical day in a civilized society, not a typical day at all, he thought . . . *except in a society of forgotten souls.*

He looked down at his drab black shoes and easily tucked his shirt into his ill-fitting pants as a cell block guards distant commands echoed throughout the spartan cubicles.

A moment to reflect, albeit brief, as he stared through the cold, impenetrable bars that had defined his existence for nearly ten years. Ten years that had stolen his youth, his dreams and his spirit.

He wondered if his once proud name would ever be restored. He would repeat it under his breath so as not to lose his identity . . . Juan Carlos Almeda . . . Juan Carlos Almeda . . . Juan Carlos . . .

A peripheral glance toward his cellmate standing next to him revealed . . . the hint of a smile? *What would possibly stimulate a smile in this God forsaken environment..*

And so it was that two men stood side by side, anticipating the piercing buzz that would release the locking mechanism and cause the large steel barred doors to their cell to open. Two haggard men who had been mere boys when they were initially incarcerated.

When Bobby Makison and Juan Carlos Almeda came to Concord Reformatory nearly ten years ago they had been just 21 years old. Both had been aspiring engineering students at Northeastern University, just a few short years away from obtaining their degrees.

Bobby's only fear had been how to scare up his next tuition payment. Carlos . . . well, money wasn't a problem, but something else had been, something a little more serious.

They were an interesting contrast standing next to each other. Bobby was short, blonde and blue eyed. His Finnish heritage was chiseled into his features. His demeanor, quiet. When he found it necessary to speak, his words were measured, slower than those uttered by Carlos. His only problem on this particular morning were his pants . . . letting his belt out another notch. He was having no trouble putting away the bland, sometimes fatty food served up at the prison and was thinking that he'd best take up jogging in the yard during the recreational time afforded the prisoners.

Carlos was a classically handsome Cuban with light bronze skin, lean physique, brown eyes and black hair that had recently begun to show some graying at the temples. He stood little more than half a foot taller than Bobby. His personal tempo was quicker than Bobby's and the apprehension he had been experiencing during the last few weeks was making it faster. His remaining time in prison was weighing heavily on his mind.

Had he been able to read Bobby's mind he would have discovered that his perplexing smile that morning was a smile of hope. A dream that had sustained him for a decade was coming closer to reality . . . his parole hearing.

Standing next to his best friend, Bobby's thoughts drifted back to happier times.

They had known each other at Northeastern. Carlos had a room across the hall from him in a rooming house on St. Botolph Street in Boston's Back Bay, a few blocks from the university.

Carlos was supposed to be studying mechanical engineering, but it always appeared to Bobby that he was working toward a PHD in Female Anatomy. Some of the most beautiful women in Boston were over there almost every night, and the sounds of Tito Puente constantly filled his room. There was very often a little spillage of sound from that room . . . and then it would become extremely quiet, except for an occasional giggle or moan.

Bobby would never forget the night that Carlos knocked on his door wanting to talk. He was usually care free and happy, but that night his face was drawn and he appeared frightened. It was a distraught Carlos that Bobby had never seen before.

"They are going to kick me out!" he replied raising his arms in a pleading manner.

"Out? What the hell do you mean, out? Maybe I can talk to the landlord and . . ."

"No, man . . . out of Northeastern!" replied Carlos angrily.

"Didn't you just tell me your GPA was 2.7?" asked Bobby.

"Yes, but I flunked several English related courses, and that is why, my friend."

Carlos slumped in a chair holding his head between his hands.

"Hell's bells, man. Isn't there somebody you can talk to, Carlos?" asked Bobby as he noticed a letter protruding from Carlos's shirt pocket.

"I just did, amigo. I just came from the Dean's office. I tried to explain that my visa will automatically expire if they terminate me. You know that I cannot go back to Cuba, Bobby, not now!"

Carlos's father was a prominent doctor and friend of President Fulgencio Batista of Cuba.

"I might be a very dead hombre if they deport me now, Bobby. I do not know where my family is right now," Carlos lamented as he showed Bobby the letter that had made a bad day even worse.

December 23, 1958

My Dear Juan Carlos:

The situation here in Cuba is very grave. The celebration of the birth of our Holy Savior is far from

11

our minds. The country has essentially been cut into two pieces by the Castro forces.

We have heard this day that Che Guavera, one of his commanders, has captured Fomento, Cabaiguan and Guayos, and is approaching Havana with his army. Thus far, the government forces have not been effective in stopping his advance.

I have decided that it will be no longer safe for us here in Marianao, and I have already made arrangements for your mother, sister and myself to leave the country.

As you know, we have consistently supported our Presidente's leadership, and it is no secret that atrocities have already been committed against his compatriots. I can take no chances.

Grandmama and grandpapa have decided to stay. Nothing I can say will dissuade them. They will attempt to return to Cienfuegos, their hometown, where they have friends.

Juan Carlos, I fear that you will never see your home again. Once we abandon it we will only be left with our fond memories of our life there. I only pray that, someday, we will all be able to return together.

I cannot tell you where we will go at this time, but I will contact you again as soon as I possibly can.

Thank God that you are safe from all of this. Please continue to take care of yourself, study hard, and do not worry about us.

Daria mi propia vida por ellos!

Love,
Papa

Words would not come as Bobby looked down at Carlos after reading the letter. He slumped to a seated position on the floor across from Carlos trying hard to fight back the approaching tears that had begun to gloss his eyes.

Casually wiping his sleeve across his eyes to absorb any moisture that might reveal his sadness he gazed at a remote corner of the room while trying to gather his thoughts. What could he possibly say to downplay the devastating news that he had just been entrusted with.

He was hoping that both situations couldn't possibly be as grim as they had been portrayed. His mind groped vainly for something that he might be able to suggest, when Carlos suddenly relieved him from uttering what would have been a banal reply at best.

"What do you say we get the fuck out of here, my friend? Would you join me in seeking out a happier climate where we can temporarily forget about this turn of events?"

Bobby's mood was instantly broken. Relieved that he had been rescued from his dilemma, but more shocked because he had never heard his mild mannered, soft spoken friend utter so much as a four letter word before. Sure, he had a quiz tomorrow in Hydraulics, but studying could wait , and he had a feeling that he knew what Carlos had in mind.

* * *

He had taken Bobby and a few of his friends around on the Latin nightclub circuit once before, and though Bobby liked the music, he wasn't a big drinker and he felt a little out of place. That night, however, it definitely seemed like the thing to do.

"Maybe I can scare us up a little tender Cuban pussy, Mr. Bob. Maybe I do not know how much time I have left in your Boston," as the beautiful smile that had won Carlos more than a few women's hearts came across his handsome face.

Bobby couldn't help but think that Carlos's dire forecast of time remaining in Boston was a little premature, but he

8-MAKI

had little doubt regarding his ability to find women. His immediate concern was how these women might take to him.

They made an interesting pair as they walked up Huntington Avenue over to Stuart Street and headed toward the South End.

On the way by 'The Stables Bar' near the Boston Public Library Bobby tried to get Carlos to go in with him to catch a set of his favorite music, jazz, but looking in the front door at the long bar that led to the ramp down to where Herb Pomeroy's band played, Carlos could see no women.

As they passed a club called 'Jacques', Bobby related to Carlos that it was the first place in Boston that he and some friends had been served a beer several years before when they were slightly under age.

"We all walked in and sat in a booth. The waiter eyed us suspiciously, but he served us. Then he went to the next booth where one of the men stood up and kissed the waiter smack on the lips. When we saw the parade of guys going in and coming out of both the Men's and Women's Rooms we finally got the message. We chug-a-lugged our beers fast and got the hell out of there," laughed Bobby as he looked over his shoulder.

"Small town boy meets sin city, Mr. Bob?" Carlos replied. "We had the same in Havana. They don't really bother anybody. Some day they will find a place in the community because they are intelligent, caring and productive people who also need to have some fun."

Bobby was momentarily taken aback by Carlos's liberal lecture on morality, but just as they rounded the next corner you could hear their destination before you could see it. The music was infectious.

Two huge Cubans were stationed just outside the door to the club. Bobby remembered thinking that their muscular development might have detracted from their flexibility, but he sure didn't want to test any of their attributes. He was relieved when they both broke into smiles upon seeing Carlos.

Their smiles became somewhat tainted with curiosity when they saw him, however.

"Buenas noches, mi amigo!" one of them replied to Carlos as they slowly parted like the loading doors to a ferry.

Carlos returned the greeting as he and Bobby strode into the noisy, smoke filled club. The bar was literally lined with customers, but Carlos quickly caught the eye of one of the female bartenders wearing snuggly fitting satin shorts and a tight fitting black brocade top that left nothing to the imagination. Her brief look at Carlos was enough to reveal the hint of a past relationship as she complied with his request for two rum cokes and several cigars. As she mixed the drinks they exchanged brief, telling glances.

It was as though Carlos knew everyone in the room. It was truly Cuba in a little part of Boston, a safe refuge and a feeling of home for him.

As Bobby scanned the club he couldn't help thinking what the devil a handsome, personable, extroverted guy like Carlos was wasting his time studying engineering anyway. Hell, everyone knew that engineers were generally introverted, quiet loners whose secret wish was to be locked in a room full of technical books with their slide rules and a pot of coffee. Most were even downright nerdy. Bobby hoped he didn't quite fit the stereotype. He damn well knew that Carlos didn't.

The first drink went down quickly, and before they had finished the next one, Carlos had already made the acquaintance of two beautiful, dark haired, brown eyed lovelies. Problem was, Bobby sensed they both had the hots for Carlos.

A few words were exchanged in Spanish between Carlos and the more statuesque of the two as Bobby noticed her slide her sequined purse along the table top toward Carlos.

At that same moment, Bobby was distracted by the stare of her friend. She had a smile on her face, and it almost appeared to be saying, "Actually, he's kind of a cute little gringo. Maybe he wouldn't be so bad after all?"

Bobby cautiously returned her smile, and then looked at Carlos.

"Maybe the girls would like to go back to 'The Stables' with us. We could catch a set, pick up some more juice, and make it back to your pad for some more cha cha action."

Somehow the suggestion seemed to get lost in a maze of blank stares and louder Latin music. In fact, the expression on the face of the girl that had been watching him became so quizzical, he wasn't at all sure she had understood any of what he had said.

In the meantime, Carlos had slid something out of the purse in front of him, under his palm.

"Mr. Bob?" he said. "What do you say we take a little walk. I have something I want you to try."

Bobby was becoming so rum relaxed that he didn't have a clue what Carlos was talking about, but whatever it was, the girls apparently knew, because they were looking at each other having a good giggle.

Carlos stood up, grabbed him by the arm and headed across the crowded dance floor toward the Men's Room weaving around the ebullient couples who appeared to be attached by unseen elastic bands. Bobby was definitely in tow until Carlos lost his grip bumping into someone near the door, but when he entered, Bobby was only a few steps behind.

There was a swinging door just inside the door labeled 'Senore' and Carlos hit it so hard and fast that it met with some resistance as it swung. He was about to apologize to the man it had hit when he saw a gun go skidding across the tile floor and what looked like a silencer bounce across the floor to be caught between the legs of a completely inanimate and totally dead figure sitting in a urinal.

The dead man had apparently turned around while relieving himself only to be hit in the forehead by the assassin's bullet. His bladder valve obviously hadn't had time to get the message before his brains had been relocated onto the wall because his penis was still excreting urine onto the floor. The silencer looked like a sinister phallic symbol as it rolled to a stop between his legs. You could just make out some cellophane bags containing a white substance taped to his legs just above his socks.

"Holy shit, Carlos! Look out! yelled Bobby as the man that had been knocked to the floor by the impact of the swinging door got up with a long, striated switchblade in his hand and proceeded toward Carlos menacingly.

He was a very large Negro with pitch black skin, a nose that looked like it had been broken by a frying pan and several gold earrings in each ear. Dick Butkis might have been able to bring him down in his prime, minus the knife. Blood was dripping from a wound to the back of his left hand apparently made by the door as he transferred the knife to his right hand and unsteadily walked toward Carlos.

The dead man on the floor appeared to be of Latin heritage with lighter skin, close cropped hair and a pencil thin moustache. His frontal appearance had only been marred by the small, almost undiscernable bullet hole in the center of his forehead.

"Bobby! Get the gun! Get the gun!" screamed Carlos with both arms raised at shoulder height looking for something, anything he might pick up and hurl at the oncoming killer. There was nothing.

The gun had finally ended up in a stall, almost in back of a toilet. Bobby felt a sudden rush of adrenaline negate the alcohol he had consumed as he dove under the stall door and picked up the gun. It was an old Army 45, but the clip had fallen out and was several feet away.

He turned, with gun in hand, only to see Carlos receive a shallow but painful trust to the chest. There was no time to reach for the clip. If there was no bullet in the chamber, Carlos was probably a dead man, and he was too.

The gun felt huge in his small hand, so he used both hands, aimed and fired, just as the Negro was about to make a horizontal thrust directed at Carlos's heart. The thrust went through the meaty part of Carlos's hand as he vainly attempted to block it. A split second later the chambered bullet entered between the black man's shoulder blades and blew out his sternum. He slumped forward with a quizzical look on his face, missing Carlos by inches.

"Yeii!!" Carlos yelled in pain. "Bobby! What happened here? What have we done?"

At that moment the room started spinning, and Bobby was suddenly feeling very ill. All that he had seen and experienced during the past few minutes was hitting him like year old yogurt. In an instant, he lost his stomach contents.

People out in the club had heard the shot. Some began cautiously peering in.

Men began shouting 'policia'! Women began screaming. A sizeable crowd was congregating at the door effectively blocking it. There appeared to be no way out.

CHAPTER TWO

The sudden combative shrill of two alley cats pierced the quiet night air rousing Monahan from inevitable slumber. As he gathered his nerves together only the subdued sounds of patrons in the Latino Club could be heard.

He ran his index finger under the tight collar of his polyester shirt as a bead of sweat slid slowly from his forehead to his cheek. Nothing fit right anymore, he lamented, but his civies were a damn site more comfortable than his old uniform.

Dammit, I should have called Heniger on this caper, thought Monihan. *Captain Brady better cover my ass or I'm dead meat.*

He didn't like working with the high and mighty Feds anyway and the Captain's point was well taken. How could we be sure what we were dealing with tonight?

Young Jim Heniger was one of those ambitious up and comers with the Boston office of the FBI. His obvious zeal had landed him the position as head of the task force dealing with drugs, particularly coming out of Cuba.

It was with some reluctance that he had accepted the assignment of Boston Police Department liaison with Heniger's unit, but money talks and the extra cash resulting from his promotion was hard to pass up, not to mention the hike in pension benefits that would accrue. Besides, he had worked hundreds of stakeouts during his career, most of them related to drug activity. It was the new burgeoning evil in Boston.

He was supposed to call Heniger on this one, but he knew Brady was tired of sharing the spotlight with the FBI and

having them pick up most of the credit for the busts, so . . .
he just did what he was told and never picked up the phone.
Nothing like being caught between a big rock and hard place,
he thought.

There was a time when the twenty three year veteran of the
force might have been described as robust, but in recent years
the sands of time had begun to shift. His blood pressure was
not good and his ruddy red face was always a good indicator
of the varying hues of his disposition.

His right arm was the only part of his anatomy that he
exercised daily as he hoisted his beer mug with the boys at
Duggan's Bar in Southie, mostly after his shift. However, he
was known to stop in and down a few quick ones on a warm
day while on duty.

It had been well known that many of the musicians playing
gigs around the city had been users since the late forties, but
drug activity had really started to pick up during the fifties.

A few months before Fidel Castro became a serious threat
to Batista, there had been large quantities of some very pure
coke smuggled out of Cuba. Some of it was coming out with
the substantial criminal element who were fleeing like rats
from a sinking ship. They had been monitoring Castro's frequent speeches from the Sierra Maestra in which he had made
it quite clear that he would not tolerate crime, gambling or
prostitution, all of which flourished under the Batista regime.

Monahan and his partner Manny Diaz had been assigned to
head up a task force out of the local precinct on Berkeley Street.
It didn't include Scollay Square, but it was a pretty hot area of
the city including the Commons, the Combat Zone and part of
the Back Bay over to Columbus Avenue. A rough beat that included most of the nightclubs and a few that did a high volume
business like the Hillbilly Ranch and the Boston Club.

"Man, I hope this shitbox can move out when we need
it," said Diaz to Monahan as they peered down the alley from

inside their unmarked fifty seven Chevy. "This place gives me the creeps."

"Don't worry, the guys in the shop tell me they put more than a few stallions under the hood," said Monahan as he glanced over at his temporary partner noticing his immaculately fitting uniform. "You'd better take off that god damn hat or somebody's going to make us out here, pretty boy."

Diaz had been pulled off his beat around the South End because he knew the territory and spoke fluent Spanish. He had gotten the word through his informants that something big was going down at the Latino Club that night. No details, no who, no what, no nothing.

He wasn't at all comfortable working with Monahan. He knew he was a demeaning son-of-a-bitch. He often sensed that Monahan just didn't like hispanics . . . or blacks . . . or orientals, or anybody that didn't come from Southie for that matter.

It had been a tough pull for Diaz to withstand the discrimination that existed on the police department and he wondered if it would ever change.

There was little question that he would rather be amongst his own people, but he had been successful at establishing his own little niche amongst the predominantly Irish constabulary. There had been times when he had to take a huge gulp of pride to fit in, but it didn't detract from his self respect and abilities as a police officer and as a leader in his own community. He knew, deep down, that in spite of his slightly diminutive size, he was still faster and smarter than most.

"Just think, I could have been sittin' in the Garden right now." said Monahan.

"De Bruins playin' tonight?" asked Diaz.

"Naah . . . watchin' them fairies dance around the ice with the Ice Capades. I was supposed to take the kids. My wife took 'em instead."

-MAKI

"You are a fortunate son-of-a-bitch, you know that? I mean, here we are sittin' in this rat infested alley havin' a much betta' time," replied Diaz.

"O.k., o.k., so I left myself open for that one."

"Yeah, you did, my bone headed 'mick' friend," replied Diaz. "I myself would have gone to the Sportsman's Show at Mechanics Hall. Teddy Williams was gonna be over there demonstrating some fly casting. He's quite a fisherman when he ain't playing ball you know."

"Man, if he fishes like he hits the ball, he could open his own fish market. I figure he's got a few more years. What do you think?" asked Monahan.

"I don't know , he could be close to trowin' in de towel. Hey, how bout dis kid Yamenski? . . . Yasminski? What de hell's his name?" asked Diaz while digging through his shirt pocket.

"Yastremski, for Christ's sake. Carl Yastremski. I think he could be good," said Monahan. "But nobody's gonna fill the 'Splinter's' shoes."

Diaz pulled a pack of 'Luckys' from his pocket.

"If you gotta light one of those fucking things, make sure you do it under the goddam . . ."

Before Monahan got the word 'dash' out of his mouth, a shot rang out inside the club.

"Cover the back door , Manny! I'll go in from the front entrance," Monahan said as Manny grabbed his nightstick and jumped out.

Monahan burned rubber and took off down the alley.

Inside the club Bobby's head had finally stopped spinning, and he had no more stomach contents to give.

"Carlos! We've got to get out of here fast !" he said as he was down on all fours looking for an exit. His head was swaying like a newborn calf in a corral, almost afraid to find out if his legs worked.

"There's some kind of door over there," Bobby said pointing with his head.

The door had obviously not been opened for a long time because the deadbolt was severely rusted.

Carlos was bleeding badly as he pried the knife from the Negro's death grip and attempted to jimmy the deadbolt loose.

Just as Bobby was standing up he couldn't help but notice a rather large briefcase on top of the urinal where the Latino had been murdered. It was made of exquisite brown leather and it's brass clasps shined as they caught the light from the cheap overhead fluorescent lights. It looked strangely alluring. Impulsively he ran over and grabbed it.

Diaz had been squatting by the back door leading from the kitchen to the alley. When he heard the deadbolt release from the Men's Room some twenty feet away he jumped up just in time to see it open.

Carlos hit the door opening first and Diaz swung his night stick. He caught Carlos across the left tibia.

Bobby could actually hear the bone break and Carlos was down writhing in pain as Diaz jumped on his back and fumbled to remove the handcuffs from his belt.

He had leaped over the two of them and was already far down the alley. He looked back for an instant to see if he could help his friend. Unknown to him, Carlos was going into shock from the excruciating pain, and as he was passing out, his last words began to sound like someone putting their thumb on a spinning forty-five rpm record.

"Go! Go! Go! Bobby . . . run . . ." Carlos mumbled not even realizing he had spoken his good friend's name.

Impulsively, Bobby turned and ran like hell.

Diaz finally got the cuffs on Carlos, drew his thirty-eight, and whistled a shot just over Bobby's shoulder.

The briefcase was heavy and cumbersome, and he wondered why he had even taken it, except for thought of what it might contain. He had tried to flip the lock just after he picked it up, but it was locked.

God, he was sick and tired, and more scared than he had ever been in his life. He ran blindly. All he knew was that he was approaching the Boston Common.

Panic drove him. He had just killed a man. A man who had apparently been involved in some kind of drug deal.

He slowed down just enough so as not to draw attention. There were more people in the streets now.

Got to get rid of this thing, he thought, *but if it has something in it, I just can't throw it away, not after all they had been through.*

He was walking past the Statler Hotel when he remembered the Motor Mart Building where his dad had always parked his car when they drove to Boston.

There it was, just up ahead. There must be someplace in that dark, scary place where he could hide the briefcase. He remembered how nervous he used to get when his dad drove his wide old Buick up the narrow, winding ramps between floors.

When he entered the stairwell door on the street level he was so exhausted he hardly noticed the pungent urine smell always prevalent. He headed up the stairway until his legs gave out on the third floor.

He cautiously opened the door to the parking area. There appeared to be no one on the floor. The theater crowd had filled up the parking spaces a few hours ago and they shouldn't return for another hour or so.

Where . . . where? he thought as he looked around. He had never realized how spartan parking garages were.

Nothing . . . no possible hiding places here, he mumbled softly to himself, and then he looked up. The ceiling was odd looking, like a concrete honeycomb. It was the same 'pan construction' that he learned about in one of his concrete design courses. Good old Professor Spensor. The forms are shaped like little sinks with recesses between them. *So what? How the hell do I get up there?*

How about where a pan intersects with a stairwell? he thought, as he headed for one.

Around the backside of the stairwell fronting the street he spied a potential cache. If he could climb the heavy window frame, he could access it.

Just then he heard voices below him in the well. A young family was obviously returning from an early movie or late supper.

Christ, what now? Bobby thought, as he ducked between two parked cars, hoping that one of them didn't belong to them.

He guessed right on the cars, but not where the family had been. They were talking about a jazz concert they had just attended at the Arlington Street Church. He couldn't help thinking he might have enjoyed that concert and would have been a hell of a lot better off.

After they drove the car down the ramp he cautiously climbed the window framework with the briefcase and crammed it into a crevice where it could be supported on a small ledge on the stairwell exterior. It couldn't fall and unless you were staring directly at it, you could barely make out the rippled bottom of the case.

Now what? Got to get back to the pad, he thought , *pick up some clothes. Maybe go home for a few days. There must be a way out of this mess.*

It was a long walk back to St. Botolph Street. He would pass the 'Stables' jazz club for the second time in one evening without going in. Tonight he had other things on his mind. Very serious things.

Could he have helped Carlos? No, he was sure he couldn't. Carlos would need medical attention in a hurry. Was it a cop who hit him coming out? It must have been.

Why else would he have shot at me? Yeah they would probably take him to Boston City Hospital. He would be cared for. What was in that damn briefcase? Had the cop seen him carry it out?

As he walked past Joe and Nemo's and turned left on Massachusetts Avenue he had a pretty good idea there was no way out. They even knew his name. He was physically and mentally exhausted.

Crusher Casey's bar was doing their typical booming business as he walked past and took a left on St. Botolph Street. He could tell that Northeastern had just finished playing hockey at the Arena and had probably won, judging by the happy mood of the kids pouring out onto the street.

There was little doubt that he would now give himself up and he would not abandon Carlos. He'd do his best to explain how the entire bazaar evening had unfolded, but first he needed to lie down, if only just for a few minutes.

He slowly walked up the steps to the old brownstone where he and Carlos lived and suddenly felt the pressure of a gun barrel thrust into his rib cage as soon as he opened the ornate glass door.

"You have the right to remain silent..."

*   *   *

It took three months for their trial to come up. During that entire time Bobby never saw Carlos. They had been isolated in separate detention facilities. One of their defense attorneys did divulge that his leg was still in a cast and his knife wounds were healing nicely. She also said that Carlos had been asking about him.

Unfortunately, incriminating evidence was piling up. Their fingerprints had been found on both the gun and the knife, and the police had found a small bag of coke on Carlos similar to the coke found on one of the dead men.

Over the course of trial preparation no less than three public defenders worked on the case. It was turning out to be a debacle and there was no money available for an experienced attorney.

Carlos's affluent family was still in hiding somewhere and completely unaware of what had happened, and Bobby's family was completely out of the picture.

When the trial eventually came up they were defended, at the last minute, by an older attorney they had rarely seen. Most of the attorneys in the Public Defender's Office were generally young go-getters who were out to make a name for themselves before they struck out on their own. This particular attorney had worked primarily as a trust and estate lawyer for most of his career. Rumor had it that his political connections had landed him this assignment.

The trial lasted only four days and the experienced prosecutors ate the defense alive. The jury deliberated two short hours. The verdict was guilty on two counts, possession with intent to distribute a controlled substance and second degree murder.

The judge imposed twenty year sentences with eligibility for parole in ten. They were to serve their time at Concord Reformatory in Massachusetts.

The sentences were considered by most to be extremely harsh considering the circumstances, but were imposed, in part, to reflect the new get tough policy regarding drug trafficking in the city.

Throughout the trial the question regarding the absence of the money used for the drug buy had continually come up. Police investigators had speculated that the money hadn't arrived by the time the killings took place and the carrier might have been alerted. The preponderance of evidence was used very effectively to prove that Bobby and Carlos had killed the Negro, were in possession, and in on the buy.

Several times during the trial Bobby had thought about the possibility of using his knowledge of where the briefcase was to cop a plea, but decided such a confession might actually work against them. What would it prove, and what if it were just filled with old newspapers?

While waiting for the trial he became obsessed with what that briefcase might contain and ultimately decided to test his odds at personally finding out some day. Incredibly, no one, not even Carlos knew that he had lugged it out of the bloody Men's Room that night.

Bobby vowed that he would tell his good friend, if, and when the opportunity ever presented itself to return to the Motor Mart Building.

CHAPTER THREE

Nearly ten years later and some forty miles west of Concord Reformatory on a clear, cold, blustery spring morning it was opening day once again.

Alan Makison had made the drive from his modest split ranch house to the Hillston Municipal Golf Course for the past eight years.

As his car bounced through one of the many potholes caused by the recent spring thaw he wondered how he had ever adapted to weathering the constant complaints and fickle desires of the general public without going completely mad.

All he had ever wanted to do was play golf... professional golf on tour, and dammit, he had been good. He had been good since he could walk. It had started with raw, natural athletic ability and been refined by some excellent teachers.

Sure, he had been temperamental, but most often it would work to his advantage. Early on, it had fueled his competitiveness. He had won the club championship at Hillston Municipal four times, in addition to several state titles. He had turned professional and successfully qualified for the PGA Tour.

During the New Orleans Open he had sunk a phenomenal forty-foot putt on the final hole to edge Lee Trevino for the top spot and the $40,000 purse. He had had the world by the tail, but would soon lose his grip. In fact, it might have proved better if he had never tasted success at all.

As he drove to the golf course that morning his mind drifted back a decade. It almost seemed as if it had been a dream.

That press party he had thrown following the win at New Orleans had been talked about for months afterward. Sure, it had taken a healthy bite out of the winner's check along with taxes, and his hungry sponsors getting some of their long overdue investment returned, but it had been a sweet victory. A victory to build upon. He and Judy would ride the high all the way to the next tournament way up in Philadelphia.

Yes, it was all coming back to him again, and he could remember saying . . .

"Honey, can you believe it! I don't have to qualify for any of the remaining tournaments for the rest of the year!"

"I'm so proud of you Alan. You've worked so hard for this. I love you very much," Judy had said as she threw her arms around him and kissed him . . . again . . . and again. He still remembered lying with her in bed, sharing her love.

She had never complained about traipsing around the country in their broken down Nash Rambler, staying in flea bag motels and eating fast food. Not to mention his frequent mood swings.

Life on the tour can be downright tough for the 'rabbits'. The little perks don't really start coming until you attain a little name recognition with that first win. Some never see a hint of success, very quickly run out of money, and head back home to accept a local club job.

"Wait 'till you see this place I made a reservation for in Philly, honey," said Alan. "No more outhouses for us, kid. We're on our way up!"

There were times, Judy thought, that Alan need only spread out his arms and fly, he exuded so much confidence.

"We've still got to be careful with what little nest egg we have, Alan," Judy said as she watched him pack, but she could see that she had been talking to the wall. Alan's mind was already on the next tournament.

* * *

It had been cold up in Philly. Usually when the tour starts moving north in early summer it starts to warm up, but not that year.

Alan wore a turtleneck and a sweater for most of the first two rounds of the tournament, but his game was still sharp from New Orleans, and he was only two shots off the pace.

The weather turned even colder for the third round, and he found himself constantly blowing into his hands because of his inherently poor circulation.

He had been fortunate to pick up one of the tour's more experienced caddies for the tournament. Mo Johnson, a seasoned bag toter had caddied for the best. His favorite stories were about 'The Iceman', Ben Hogan, who he had caddied for just following his return from the tragic automobile accident that almost ended his career. Needless to say, many of his stories centered around 'Gentle Ben's' determination and courage.

He told no tales on the golf course though. He was there to provide the best information he could to his pro. After all, his pro's success would be reflected in his paycheck following the tournament.

Early on, during the third round, Alan had been having a difficult time keeping his hands warm. He shoved them into his pockets walking up to the third tee. Upon reaching the tee he blew into them again, slipped his glove on, and pulled his Driver out of his bag.

Mo never flinched when Alan began taking a few practice swings with his Driver to loosen up. He would have recommended the same club because he had been hitting the ball with radar accuracy off the tee with it for the entire tournament. In fact he had only missed one fairway during the past three days of competition.

The third hole was a relatively short, but narrow par four. It was bordered by trees on the left and a rock strewn swale on the right. There was only one acceptable place to make a viable shot to the green, and that was in the middle of the fairway. It wasn't much more than a wedge shot to the green, if you could hit the ball 260 off the tee like Alan could.

Alan took a few more deliberate practice swings, looked down the fairway and let it fly.

"Shit!" he mumbled as he followed through. He knew without looking up that he hadn't gotten his hands through the shot properly. There was only one direction it could have gone . . . to the right.

When he and Mo got down to where the ball had disappeared, the spotter had already found it nestled down in the deep rough in the swale next to a rock.

"Christ, Mo! How am I gonna get the friggin' ball outta here?" asked a very aggravated Alan.

"That 'mother' looks borderline unplayable to me, man." Mo replied.

"Dammit, I almost think I can slip a wedge behind it and pop it out, providing I can get by the rock next to it. Might even be able to get it on the green somewhere, " said Alan, as his undeniable confidence was rearing it's ugly head.

"Your the boss, Mr. Alan. You know what you can do. I only know I don't like it. I'd take the drop and try to make it up on the next hole."

Alan was undeterred. He could almost picture the ball flying out onto the green.

"What have we got from here, Mo?" he calmly asked.

"One-twenty to the front. One thirty-one to the pin," Mo replied, having flipped through his little note pad containing the distances to all the pins.

Alan pulled his Sand Wedge out of his bag while Mo motioned up to the Marshal to move a few spectators that were standing too close to the intended line of flight. He knew there was no way he could get close to the pin because it was tucked too far to the right behind a trap, but hitting the green was at least a possibility.

He took his stance and fidgeted for a long time trying to set his feet comfortably, looked up at the green a final time to picture the shot in his mind and then swung.

The next thing he remembered was Mo asking, "You all right, man?" and then it seemed as though all the pain he had ever endured in his life had been saved, packaged up, and suddenly untied. He must have blacked out for a few seconds, but he was still on his feet, awake and looking at the headless shaft in his left hand. His right hand hung limp as the broken bone tried unsuccessfully to exit through the skin.

He had figured everything but the piece of ledge directly under the ball that he hadn't been able to see.

His wrist never did heal correctly because of the nerve damage that had occurred, and though he had attempted a comeback after several months he couldn't get the feeling back in his right hand and the painkillers dulled his concentration.

Even though he had been exempt from qualifying for the remainder of the year, he began missing cuts, not by just a little, but by ten strokes and more. Medical and travel expenses had just about exhausted their hard earned nest egg, and to Judy's dismay he began drinking heavily. By year's end, both had hit rock bottom.

He would never forget the day Judy presented her ultimatum. They were in Florida staying in a terrible motel some ten miles from the tournament site. He had just picked up a $247 check for twenty-fourth place finish. They had needed that check to settle with the motel, pay for car repairs, and barely move on to the last few tournaments that year.

In his frustration, he had stopped at the clubhouse bar for a few drinks before heading back to the motel. When he finally left he was very drunk and had barely one hundred dollars remaining in his pocket.

It was dark when he somehow found his way back to the motel. Judy knew immediately where he had been. His drunken state had actually carried him several miles past the motel, and well beyond remorse. He was disgustingly giddy when he opened the door.

"Where have you been, Alan?" she asked, breaking into tears.

Alan leaned against the doorframe for support vainly attempting to appear sober. He fumbled through his pockets only to see the few remaining dollars spill out. The smirk was now gone from his face and the depth of his despair evident. Even in his drunken state he could understand the folly of a reply to Judy's question.

"I'm going home tomorrow, Alan. I can't go on living like this . . . seeing you like this. I love you too much. I called Daddy tonight, and he's wired me some money."

Alan vaguely remembered trying to persuade her to stay before he fell across the bed.

When he finally awoke the next day soaked in sweat by the hot Southern sun shining through the only window in the room . . . she was gone.

Judy had been his high school sweetheart, his first and only love. She had shared in all his triumphs, and had finally shared in the depths of the abyss.

He read the brief note she had left, over and over again while his head pounded unmercifully. He couldn't believe what he had done. He knew he couldn't go home, not now. He needed time to think, to get his head straight. Yes, he must persuade Judy to come back. There was a bar across the street. A drink would clear his head.

Later on that afternoon, and many drinks later, he was in no better state than the previous evening. In fact, he was much worse off because he had just sold his golf clubs to an enterprising patron in the bar a few hours earlier.

What the fuck, I can't play golf with this goddam wrist anyway, so what the hell good are they, he had rationalized in his mind numbing state.

Following a few more drinks he got in his car and drove. He had no idea what direction he was headed and it was a miracle that he was never stopped and thrown into a local drunk tank.

To this day he still couldn't remember how he ever got to Pascagula, but that's where the old Nash Rambler finally gave out, and where he would eventually purchase the very same Eldo that was miraculously conveying him to Hillston Municipal on this day.

Alan made the final turn onto the winding road to the course and took a second to glance at the buds on the trees hesitating to expose their buds in the cold spring air.

He wondered as he drove about his Judy, and how different Beth was.

* * *

His courtship of Beth had been quick. After he had finally drifted back to Hillston, he had sought out one of his old sponsors, Matt Cormier. Matt had run a successful insurance business in town for years. Beth was Matt's daughter and had just graduated from a local community college with a business degree. She had been working as his secretary. Matt's wife had died a few years earlier. She had never approved of Alan.

That first evening when Alan had been invited over for dinner at the Cormier's, Beth had been there. At the time he hadn't realized how vulnerable he was. He was hurting for a new sense of stability, and even more, he was hurting for companionship.

Among other things, he had been impressed by her self assuredness and intelligence. He had also thought about what it might be like to make love to her. Was that so strange an initial compulsion, he had thought. Would she be as stiff appearing as she did at the dinner table as she quoted the latest seat belt survival statistics. Alan remembered glancing at her and wondering how she might look naked, with just a seat belt on. How it would fall between her very ample breasts.

"Alan, we are all so happy that you decided to come back home," she said with a smile that seemed to say a little more. She had often been the sounding board for her father's comments relative to Alan's exploits, and she admitted to being somewhat enamored by his brief, but exciting career, in spite of knowing absolutely nothing about golf.

"I must confess that the reason I asked you over tonight was because the local golf course is going to looking for a pro this coming season. When I heard you were in town it occurred to me that you were the ideal candidate. You might have heard that Danny O'Brien is retiring?" Matt said interrupting the infatuating glances between Beth and Alan.

The old course had never actually had a golf professional before. Danny had been more of a superintendent.

Alan had heard rumors of the retirement so he wasn't really shocked, nor was he really enthused about the prospects of being a pro at a municipal golf course. Sure, the course had some sentimental attraction. Alan had learned to play golf on the old Donald Ross layout that went up, down and around the town's reservoir called Clear Lake.

One of holes actually went right over a portion of the lake that had become the graveyard for many a golf balls, and a few sets of golf clubs. It was unquestionably one of the most picturesque courses in the county.

Alan had often reminisced about what someone with a more acute knowledge of golf might be able to do to improve the course, maybe even add another nine holes.

"I don't think it would take too much persuading on my part to convince the others on the golf course commission that you would be a particularly good candidate," he said as he looked at Beth through the corner of his eye.

Alan would have been pretty naive not to know that this pitch was coming, but he had decided that he just wasn't ready to face many of the people he had grown up with. He was almost a little embarrassed and afraid to find out how they might react to his perceived failure.

"Matt, I came here tonight to thank you for all the support you have given me over the years. In all honesty though, I guess I wanted to hear you mention the position at the course. I must tell you that, right now, I don't think I could cut it . . . psychologically, that is," Alan replied.

"I've also got to get out to Concord and visit Bobby. He needs whatever support I can give him, not to mention our dad whose sick again."

"Look, Alan, I know you've only been back a few weeks and we all sympathize with Bobby's situation. He was a great kid. Please take as much time as you need before you make your decision," pleaded Matt.

Beth had appeared somewhat nonplused over the decision regarding the position at the course, but not about Alan. He had caught her eyes on several occasions during the conversation, and they seemed to be telling him that she would like to see more of him.

When Alan left that evening he had promised Matt that he would seriously consider his offer before making any other job decisions. The simple fact was, however, he didn't really have anything else going for him.

The next day he felt compelled to give Beth a call at the office. He had to find out what else was behind those flirtatious glances.

He was hoping when he called the agency the next day that she would answer first

He was lucky. "Cormier Insurance Agency . . . may I help you?" she asked.

"Yes, I have a rather valuable automobile and I want to make sure I have enough insurance on it."

Beth felt a rush, an unusual exhilaration that she had never experienced before, at least not with a potential client. She knew immediately who it was.

"Well, Sir, what make of automobile is it and how old is it?"

She had seen what he had driven to the house in, and she giggled.

"Madam, was that you tittering? Is this not a professional insurance office? Were you making fun of my fine Southern automobile before I even gave you the vital statistics? I assure you that I would not snicker before you gave me your vital statistics."

Alan could almost see her turn crimson over the telephone, so he followed up quickly, stifling her need to respond to his titillating comment.

"Seriously, Beth, I really enjoyed meeting you last night and I am thinking about your father's offer, but right now, I'm thinking about you."

Beth could hardly catch her breath. No man had ever stimulated this strange passion she felt throughout her body.

"Alan, I want to apologize for my behavior last evening. It must have been the wine that made me a little giddy. I've been working quite a bit lately and was a little tired, and well . . . I guess that one glass I had before dinner just . . . just made me behave inappropriately."

"You have absolutely no need to apologize for anything. The fact is, I thought you were charming and that is why I called."

"Thank you, Alan. I feel a bit better about myself. You are very kind to say that."

"Now, if you still feel you owe me something, then I feel compelled to ask if you would like to join me for dinner tonight. I was thinking of some thing elegant, like Biff's Hot Dog Stand or Dino's Spaghetti House."

Beth laughed loudly causing several customers in the office to look over at her. Cupping her hand over the telephone mouthpiece she responded, "I'd like that , Alan. I'd like that very much. If you would prefer not having to come over to the house again, I think I can finish up by five and I can meet you here."

During the next few weeks Alan would discover that there was a considerable amount of passion under her cool, business like facade. They had made love on the first date. It had been like a nuclear explosion for both of them.

They would see each other frequently. Beth enjoyed eating out, and knowing that Alan didn't have much spending money, would often treat. Then they would go back to her father's office and make love on the waiting room couch, most often on the rug when they couldn't make the couch, and a few times on her desk. Beth had fallen in love with the new golf professional at the Hillston Municipal Golf Course.

* * *

Alan snapped out of his daydream, pulled his old Eldo into one of the 'Staff Only' parking spaces and proceeded into the Pro Shop. It was already packed with eager golfers. He could tell it was going to be another twelve-hour day. All this for twenty grand a year, in addition to any profit he could make on the merchandise in his tiny shop. This is what a promising career had boiled down to.

"Where in hell are the rest of the carts?" he yelled at Jeff, his newly hired young assistant who was diplomatically attempting to explain to two burly looking truck driver types that they should have called ahead for a tee time.

"I just didn't have time to get them out of the shed. Figured we'd have enough to get started. Sorry, Pro, I guess I figured wrong," Jeff yelled back.

He had been warned that Alan had an occasional hair across his ass. He also knew full well that the only reason Alan was the head Pro was that he was still considered somewhat of a home town sports hero, and not because of his savoir faire.

Christ, he could have at least said good morning first, Jeff thought, and it wasn't just his manner. He just didn't have good sales sense either. Just about everything in the shop was overpriced. Most of the members knew they could go just about anywhere else and purchase anything cheaper, and they wouldn't have to put up with his haughty take it or leave it attitude.

Alan didn't have a clue why Jeff was so ecstatic when he said he was heading home at six o'clock that evening.

"Put the place to bed, will you kid, and don't forget to lock up the receipts, " he said as he walked out thinking that he had worked his ass off all day and hadn't even had time to swing a golf club.

CHAPTER FOUR

Over at Concord Prison Bobby hadn't swung a club all day either. Just another day of a bum rap that had Alan's worse day beat by a mile, but he had a parole hearing coming up, and he could hope.

Funny what you grab onto when you're doing a stretch. Little things that keep you going, one day at a time . . . one hour at a time.

Bobby had always had the ability to get lost in a book. He wasn't sure he was born with it or he developed it, but he had a reading skill where he could look at a book page in the middle and 'click' . . . it was his. Like taking a mental photograph.

Early on in his confinement he knew he'd never make it unless he had something else to keep his mind on, so he started reading with a passion . . . law books mostly.

He took a correspondence course from a college up in Maine for a few years and then wrote to Suffolk Law School in Boston. They were impressed and arranged a degree program that he could work on in prison. It took over seven long years, but Bobby finally earned his law degree.

Early one evening while he was brushing up on some jurisprudence in his cell he was momentarily distracted by the all to familiar step pattern of Steve Bronski as he strode down the mezzanine making cell checks..

"Quiet down in there," he yelled to a couple of soul brothers in a nearby cell who were engaged in an after hours crap game.

When good looks had been handed out, Bronski had obviously been late. His deep set, almost black eyes were partially hidden under thick, unkempt brown eyebrows and he never appeared clean shaven. His nostrils were flared out much like a pig. He was a short powerfully built man through the upper torso, but his beer belly gave away his obvious lack of conditioning. Bobby was sure he had seen his picture in the dictionary under the word 'intimidating'.

Bronski had always been more than a little harsh with Bobby over the years. He definitely wasn't what you'd call a friend. He was the kind of guy who probably could never be himself if he wasn't wearing some kind of uniform and assuming whatever authority went with it.

It was undoubtedly the reason that Bronski was such a hard ass with Bobby. He was intimidated by his intelligence and it fueled his authoritative behavior.

Carlos was already sleeping when Bronski stepped in front of their cell.

"Holy shit, how the fuck can you read with that buzz saw going?" he said looking over at Carlos's bunk.

Bobby hesitated to even make polite conversation with the crude guard, but the question had called out for some type of response, however brief.

"Steve, this guy and me have been friends for so many years, it's almost like a beautiful song," said Bobby barely glancing up from his book. It was difficult for him to even make eye contact with the ugly bastard.

Bronski was never quite sure what kind of a relationship Carlos and Bobby had going. He liked to think it might be a little on the kinky side, refusing to believe that they were simply good friends with a great deal of respect for each other.

Bobby had a sense that there was something else on Bronski's little mind because he continued to linger and he usually didn't take the time to make any conversation beyond a brief taunt or command. He tried to fake reading his book thinking that there were more than a few things he didn't like about Bronski and he never wanted to find out what the other things were.

"Hey, Bobby. I want to talk to you tomorrow. I'll see you in the library at four o'clock," Bronski uttered brusquely as he continued his cell checks raking his nightstick across adjoining cell bars.

Carlos had been awakened by Bronski's parting order and winced at the noise that resembled a monotone marimba.

"What the hell does this guy want, Carlos?" asked Bobby looking at Carlos rubbing his eyes.

"I don't know, Mr. Bob, but I would not trust him. My compadres tell me he is capable of anything," Carlos replied.

* * *

They had carved a corner out of the prison library so that Bobby could assist the prisoners with any legal questions they might have, mostly appeal type stuff. For obvious reasons he wasn't supposed to conduct any business for the prison staff, although he had extended himself a few times.

When Bronski showed up a little after four, Bobby was putting some law books on the shelf and was alone.

Bronski sat down in the chair by his desk with a grotesque smirk on his face and seemed to stare at Bobby for what seemed like an eternity.

"What can I do for you, Mr. Bronski?" Bobby asked apprehensively.

Bronski continued his intimidating stare obviously attempting to set up his next question.

"Understand you could be outta here shortly if things go well. Assuming you are able to stay out of trouble, that is."

"Trouble . . . what do you mean by that?" Bobby asked warily.

"Oh, nothing really, but you never know. By the way, what are you planning to do?" asked Bronski.

MAKI

Bobby felt like he was participating in some kind of cat and mouse game, and was damn sure which participant he was.

"I'm really not sure yet. Maybe hang out a shingle in my old home town. Do you think anybody would trust a lawyer who's an ex con? " replied Bobby. He wanted to tell him to cut out the bullshit and get to the point, but he had to be careful. He could almost feel Bronski squeezing his balls.

"Rumor has it you got a pile of dough waiting for you when you get out," said Bronski tapping his finger tips on Bobby's desk.

Bobby felt a sickness crawl into his gut, but he knew he had to play his hand with the best poker face he could put on.

Was Bronski guessing? How could he possibly know anything? No one, not even Carlos knew, even though Bobby had made up his mind from the very beginning to split whatever might be in the briefcase with Carlos . . . if it was still where he had stashed it.

"Steve, I don't think I know what you're talking about, " replied Bobby innocently.

"You know what I'm talking about you sly little bastard . . . that caper you guys were in on, " replied Bronski gruffly.

"I don't know where you got the idea there was any money involved in that unfortunate situation Carlos and I got tangled up in," replied Bobby.

At this point the cat could not longer contain himself and Bronski rose from the chair and pounded the desk yelling, "Look, asshole! Who the fuck do you think you're dealing with here, somebody who just got off the last shrimp boat? The court transcripts are public information," said Bronski through partially clenched teeth in order to keep his voice from carrying.

So that's his little game , Bobby thought. *Maybe this guy is smarter than everyone thinks he is. He's got a shakedown business going here.*

At any rate, Bobby was relieved to hear Bronski's little revelation, because it meant that he hadn't heard it from someone else. He had never doubted that the two guys who ended up very dead that night might be members of rival factions and he hoped that the Negro by the door was a lone shooter. He figured the gang that sent out the drug messenger would probably have written the deal off seeing as how the drugs were still on the Latino by the urinal.

"I know Carlos got cuffed at the scene with a small bag on him, but you, my friend . . . you were tardy. It took you almost two hours to get from the Latino Club to your room on St. Botolph Street. It should only taken about thirty minutes the way I have it figured. There was dough at the scene and you were stashing it, weren't you?" Bronski said as the smirk grew on his ugly pockmarked face.

It was clear to Bobby that this is probably what Carlos's friends had inferred. This guy has made a science out of reading and researching the reasons why many of the inmates had been incarcerated. He wondered how many times Bronski might have been successful in working within his position of authority.

"Look, Steve, I was scared shitless and still more than a little drunk. I remember getting onto Arlington Street by the Statler and running like hell. I ran until I got to the Boston Common and I remember diving into a clump of shrubs and blowing my lunch again. I must have passed out for awhile, then I headed down Boylston. That's it, that's all there is," Bobby decried hoping that he had been convincing.

Bronski pried Bobby's eyes onto his with a cynical stare.

"Nice try, jerkoff. If you think I believe that fucking little scenario, you must think I'm ready for Cousy and the Celtics. We'll pick up on this little talk again before you leave," replied an angry Bronski.

With that, he got up, kicked the chair against the desk and left in a huff.

Bobby was numb. He sat for several minutes watching the shadows of the bars on the library window move slowly across the floor in the waning light of day. He had just experienced intimidation in its crudest form, and he wondered . . . wondered if he would ever stop seeing those shadows.

* * *

Several weeks before Bobby was scheduled to be released he was advising one of his fellow prisoners in the library when Bronski interrupted. He thought for a second that this might be his final shot until he growled, "Somebody up in the visitor's center wants to see you. You'd better get your ass up there. " Still obviously upset that he hadn't been able to shake any ripe apples from Bobby's tree.

"Tell her to send her picture first," replied Bobby jokingly.

"It's some guy, wise ass," said Bronski.

Excusing himself, Bobby trudged up to the visitor's room through several sets of locked doors and when he saw who it was he couldn't believe his eyes. His big brother had actually lowered himself from his lofty golf pedestal. He had actually driven forty miles down Route 2 to see him.

"Hey there short timer, " said Alan noticing how much older Bobby appeared.

"What do you know, Pro? " replied Bobby.

" I know you're getting out of here in a few weeks. What are you planning on doing?" asked Alan.

Well, that's a fine how do you do. No how are you, or what can I do for you , Bobby thought. *All he really wants to know is where the con is going to live. Wouldn't that make good gossip in the Pro Shop.*

"Well, Al, Carlos and I have been thinking about opening a new strip joint on Miami Beach. Nothing but high type broads, you know what I mean. I'm going to run the cracker jack concession, diamond rings in every box," replied Bobby sarcastically.

Alan appeared a little indignant, but quickly cooled off , realizing that he had lead with his right and probably deserved it.

Bobby wanted to follow up by asking Alan where he had been for last ten years. Instead he changed the subject.

"How's Dad?" he asked.

"He's back up at the state hospital drying out again," said Alan.

"He just can't hack it. He's lost everything. I think that last woman he took up with even got the money from the sale of the house."

Their dad was a classic alcoholic. He had been a brilliant student in school, but his father had decreed that he was to assist him with the photography business he had established and he was pulled out of school to do just that. For over thirty years he worked at a job he hated and when their mother died, he went to hell. He tried to erase her death and a slowly failing business from his mind with booze. He tried not to think about what he might have been. In fact, he had wanted to become a doctor.

During the past fifteen years he had been admitted to the state hospital a dozen times because there had been no money to send him to one of the few private facilities specializing in alcoholism. He was usually thrown into one of the hospital buildings called 'C-Building', full of schizophrenics and manic depressives. Here he would 'dry out'. A man with a sound mind surrounded by people with every mental illness imaginable.

"They're going to keep him a little longer this time. Maybe give him a job working in the print shop," said Alan.

"Hey, I'm sorry, man. I still love that guy. Do you realize if he hadn't had a few moments of passion and love with mom, we wouldn't be here today?" said Bobby.

"Look, I didn't mean to be a prick when you came in. I really appreciate your taking the time to come out to see me. Coming to this shithole can't be a pleasant experience. I think I really might head down Miami way with Carlos. He thinks his parents are down there somewhere and I've developed a great fondness for the Cuban people through him. I might even take the Florida bar exam, if they'll let me, and set up a practice down there," Bobby went on.

Alan was careful not to display a reaction to Bobby's revelation. He was really having trouble sorting out his feelings. They were mixed, at best. He personally loved it down south. How could you not love a place you could play golf year round. He was almost a little jealous.

At the same time, he almost wished that Bobby would come home. Hillston was the type of place where people remembered you for who you were and he was really the only family he had left, his only brother. He suddenly felt a great sense of guilt that he had been so self consumed and of so little support to Bobby.

Yet, he also sensed that he was not looking through the security screen at the same boy who needed his protection when they were going to school together. He wasn't at all the same person Alan once knew. This person could take care of himself now. Ten years in prison had hardened him.

In an instant, Alan had the answer to his dilemma.

"Al, would you mind if I were to spend a few days at your place before I head south?" asked Bobby.

"I'd like that, Bobby. I'd like that very much," Alan replied.

CHAPTER FIVE

Several days later Alan was working in the Pro Shop at the golf course when the phone rang. Jeff picked it up.

"It's for you, Pro," he said.

Alan grabbed the portable phone, tucked it under his chin and continued to put some sleeves of Titleist golf balls into the display case under the register.

"Hello, this is Alan. Hello . . . hello!"

"Alan? Alan . . . it's Judy." Her voice was soft, timid.

Alan hit the top of his head backing out of the display case. The sound of her voice touched off feelings, both bitter and sweet , and a dormant desire that had been seething since he had returned home.

"Alan, are you alright? I heard a noise," Judy replied.

Jeff looked over.

"You, of all people, should know enough to keep your head down," he said, trying to be light hearted.

"Yeah . . . yeah . . . I'm fine," said Alan as he walked to a more secluded corner of the shop.

"Judy? What . . . I mean, how are you?" he blurted out.

"I'm fine, Alan. I'm so happy to hear that things have worked out for you. I hear that you even got married," she said.

"Yes, yes I did," Alan replied uncomfortably.

"Alan, I know you must be very busy, but I'd like to see you. Would you mind very much?"

"Oh? I . . . well, sure . . . sure. I'd like that," he said fighting a melange of emotions.

"Could I possibly come over this afternoon, Alan?"

Alan thought for a moment. There are still many people in town who remembered their relationship. Maybe it wouldn't be very discrete.

"Look, Judy, I've got some lessons booked this afternoon. Would you mind meeting around seven o'clock. I should have things pretty well wrapped up by then. There's an office around back of the maintenance building across the road from the Pro Shop. Could I meet you there?" he asked.

"That would be fine, Alan, just fine."

She was shaking slightly when she put the phone down just before her son Christopher came charging through the door and tossed his lunch box on the table.

"How come you didn't come outside to meet the school bus, Mom? Mrs. Jacques was wondering where you were. She wanted to know if I can have supper and sleep over with Richard tonight," he asked hopefully.

"Oh, Honey. We have to have supper a little earlier tonight because I have to meet someone and I want you to come," she replied.

"But Mom! " Richard wants to show me his new video game. Please, Mom?" Christopher pleaded.

"I'm sorry Dear, but you'll just have to wait until tomorrow. This is very important to your mother. Do you understand?" Judy replied choking back some tears.

"You all right, Mom?" he asked, noticing a quiver in her normally firm voice as she turned away from him.

"Yes Dear, I'm fine,"

But Judy wasn't fine. She had promised herself she would never see Alan again. She had returned home to her loving parents, and Christopher had been born seven months later. She had finally found peace in her life, thoroughly enjoying her role as a mother.

She had attempted to find out where and how Alan was. He had simply disappeared and had never written.

She had desperately tried to recall the good times and tender moments, but they had always become clouded by the sad and hurtful experiences they had shared. For the longest time she wondered if she had made the right decision.

A few days before Christopher's sixth birthday her dad had collapsed mowing the lawn from a massive coronary. He had been only forty-nine years old. Judy and her mother had been devastated. He had always boasted about how healthy he was and how his father had lived to be eighty-two. He had continually failed to heed Judy's pleadings to stop, or at least cut down on the two packs of cigarettes he had smoked each day.

Judy's mother had not accepted her husband's death. She became depressed and moody. Judy spent hours trying to console her. Her doctor had said that her prolonged grieving might have contributed to the onset of her breast cancer. He said that a recent study had presented evidence of that possibility.

Judy knew that her mother had kept the lump in her breast a secret too long. The cancer had already metastasized when they discovered it. It had found its insidious route through her lymph nodes into her bones and blood. The prognosis was grim, six months to two years. A radical mastectomy was performed, followed by radiation therapy and chemotherapy.

Judy was the only one who could take her mother to the treatments and she would take Christopher along. It seemed to her that the treatments were worse than the cure . . . if there was to be a cure. Her mother could not eat for days following the treatments because of the nausea. Her own health seemed to be deteriorating. She had become a full time nurse and psychologist in addition to her role as a mother.

To make matters worse, her father had always steadfastly believed that life insurance was unnecessary and too costly. The state would provide. Funeral expenses for him had wiped out a good piece of their savings and her mother's medical bills had forced Judy to take out an equity loan on their home.

MAKI

Finally, Judy had come to the realization that she must tell Alan he had a son. She needed Alan to confide in, she had no one else.

* * *

Was there any way that Alan could have refused Judy's request for a rendezvous? He thought not. But why now? What was it that she so urgently wanted to discuss? A beautiful young woman like her would surely have found a new relationship. He could feel the guilt building again, but it was mixed with a strange, happy anxiety.

"Hey, Pro. You got a promise tonight or something? You're looking mighty happy," Jeff kidded.

Alan ignored him.

"By the way, did you get those new grips put on Mrs. Wheeler's irons. She's coming in at five to pick them up," he asked Jeff.

Jesus, had he been so transparent to solicit such a comment from a young assistant pro who spent half the day combing his own hair trying to impress every female who walked in the door?

Just before seven that evening he told Jeff to close up the shop at eight.

"I'm going across the street to pick something up and then I'm heading home, " he said.

The maintenance crew had gone home several hours ago and the shop was vacant. Alan drove his car around in back of the office and went in. In a few minutes he heard another car drive up and the motor shut off. His heart started to pound.

He was sitting behind the only desk in the office when she walked in. He had never remembered her looking so lovely. The last ten years had not been unkind.

Though she looked tired, the tiny lines she had developed made her eyes seem more alluring. Her figure was fuller and more perfectly proportioned. She was wearing a simple white sleeveless blouse and jeans. The blouse exposed her exquisite shoulders and soft, but taut upper arms. He immediately remembered the kisses that would start on those shoulders and progress up along her long neck to ultimately reach her perfectly formed lips. Her eyes were deep blue and her hair was black, though her skin was light complected. Part French-Canadian and part Swedish, a combination that had produced a stunning result.

Alan suppressed an overwhelming temptation to embrace her and tell her he was sorry. Her disarming entry caused him to quickly allay what was to have been a cooler greeting.

"Judy . . . Judy, how are you? Please sit down and tell me what you have been doing," he said nervously.

* * *

Had Alan's hand been on Judy's chest he would have felt her heart almost jump from her body as she entered the office. It was extremely difficult for her to suppress breaking into tears because of her exhaustion. She knew she would always love him in spite of the trying times she had endured living with him.

She sensed that he had lost some of his assuredness and there was a hurt reflecting from his eyes that she had never seen before, but he had kept himself in excellent shape. Except for the slight hint of grey at his temples he looked much the same as she had tried to remember him.

She had decided that she would not intrude into his new life. She would simply tell him what she had been doing, introduce him to his new son, and leave. That would be that.

Judy couldn't sit down, she was too nervous and her mind raced as she thought of how she might condense all that had happened.

"I tried to find you, Alan. I mean, after I got back home and realized what I had done. I guess I wanted to apologize," she said attempting to put her hands into her snug jean pockets. She began to pace, looking down at the floor, wondering what might happen if her eyes met his.

"By the way, you look well. You must be very happy now, being back home that is . . . and being married," she said as their eyes finally met.

Alan got up from behind the desk and walked toward her.

"I thought I was until I saw you come in just now," he replied as he reached out to embrace her.

"No, please Alan! I have some things to tell you and I don't have much time," Judy said as she glanced out the window.

"I left you because . . . well, because I just couldn't stand to see what you were doing to yourself, and . . . I left you for another reason. You see, I was pregnant with our child," she said as she could feel herself starting to break down.

Alan was stunned silent. His eyes began to narrow and his brow became furrowed in disbelief. The guilt that he had carried into the office was now more than he could stand and tears began to well up.

"A child! In God's name, why didn't you tell me, Judy?" he cried out.

"I couldn't . . . I just couldn't because I knew our child deserved a more secure and peaceful atmosphere in which to be born," she replied as tears began to stream down her cheeks.

"Jesus, Judy, if you had told me then, I would have snapped out of it," he replied.

"I didn't think so then, and I still don't think so, Alan. You were so obsessed with your inability to play that I wondered sometimes that you knew I existed," Judy lamented.

"No! No! Your wrong. I loved you so much," said Alan as he wondered how many times he had forgotten to tell her.

"Alan, your son Christopher is in my car right now. I wanted you to meet him, but think you'll agree that this may not be the right place, or the right time," she said.

Alan's remorse quickly turned to excitement as he strained to catch a glimpse of the young boy who was starting to fidget in the front seat. The evening sun was causing a glare across the windshield making it almost impossible to see him.

He wanted to run out, take the boy in his arms and hug him, but he knew she was right. His son didn't know him from Adam, and even if he were told, it could be damaging.

Judy had been studying Alan as he vainly attempted to peer out through the window blinds. She would have to arrange a better meeting place.

"God, if I could only see him better. Tell me about him, please?" Alan pleaded.

When she had driven over to the golf course Judy had no idea how the impulsive rendezvous would turn out. It could only have been played by ear, she thought. Now she knew that Christopher would have to be introduced to his father at home.

"Alan, do you suppose you could come over for supper some evening?" she asked.

"Well ... yes! That would be great," Alan replied, wondering how he could work it out.

"I really must go now. Christopher is getting antsy," Judy tried to say dispassionately, but her voice betrayed her.

She was out the door before the words were barely out of her mouth.

As they were pulling out he could tell that Christopher had engaged Judy with a barrage of questions which she had begun to reply to.

Alan locked the office door, got into his car and began his ride home. His head was spinning.

"I have a son!" he shouted, and a huge smile broke on his face. His life had suddenly gained some meaning.

When he arrived home that evening Beth was not in a good mood.

"You're late, Alan," she said standing next to the kitchen table.

"You know I have school tonight. The food has been on the table for twenty minutes and now I have to reheat it. Where have you been?" she asked.

In his ecstasy Alan hadn't figured his lateness would be an issue. He felt the blood rush to his head as he quickly attempted to fabricate an answer.

"Oh, er . . . I'm sorry, Honey. The battery on one of the golf carts went dead and it was stalled right in front of the second green. We had to get it out of there before the dew busters teed off at the crack of dawn tomorrow," replied Alan.

"Well, try to be a little more considerate on my school nights, would you dear?" Beth pleaded as she brought the reheated lasagna back to the table.

"I'm sorry that I have to run, Alan. I've already eaten. I have a test tonight and I must get over to the college. You'll have to tell me about your day when I get back," she said taking a book from the counter and dashing out.

Alan knew that he would be sound asleep when she returned and she would not wake him. He always awoke at five, several hours before she prepared to leave for the office.

Their marriage had been strained during the past year. Beth had been adamant about not wanting any children right away. She wanted her Masters degree first and nothing should interfere. Besides that, she was practically running the insurance business herself during the day. Very often she would take work home and work late into the evening.

Alan had not been happy, and it wasn't just Beth's inattention to him and her professional goals. He was living in a house virtually given to them by her father who had been instrumental in getting him his job. He felt like a kept man, like he had been bought, and he didn't like it.

This evening had been like a vitamin shot. Beth's comments had rolled off his back. Tonight his old feelings had been rekindled. Sure, he had experienced guilt, but the sight of Judy and his son had made him feel alive again.

God, I've got to see Judy and Christopher again. Do I dare call her tonight? he wondered.

Just as he looked at the phone, it rang, causing every nerve in his body to vibrate.

"Hello! Hello?" he answered, his voice tense.

"Hey, Pro, it's me, Jeff. Just thought I'd call to tell you I got the shop buttoned up. Everything go o.k. over at the maintenance shop? Noticed you were over there for awhile," he asked.

"Oh . . . yah. I was looking for the damn receipt for the mower we just bought. It has to go back for repairs," said Alan.

"O.k. then, I'll see you tomorrow," Jeff said as he hung up.

Alan thought it odd that Jeff should have called. He must have seen the other car and wondered who it was. Had he seen Judy and Christopher?

Well, so what, he thought. *It's none of his damn business. The nosey young punk.*

He would definitely have to be more careful in the Pro Shop.

He picked up the phone book. *She's got to be staying at her folk's place, but what if her mother answers? What would I possibly say?*

* * *

"Mom, I was getting worried. Who were you talking to in that office? Some kind of golf person? I saw somebody looking out the window. Could we buy some golf balls? I bet I could hit one right into one of those flag holes I saw out there. Hey, are you alright , Mom? Are you crying?" asked Christopher, finally coming up for air.

"No dear, I must be allergic to something. I'm sorry I took so long. I was watching to see if you were alright," Judy replied.

"Do you think I could still go over to see Richard tonight? Hey, who was that you were talking to anyway? Was that his car? Boy, that was a big old car."

"That was an old friend I knew before you were born, Christopher. I promise you will meet him someday soon. Now, it's getting late and we've got to get home because you have school tomorrow young man. Would you like to stop at Friendly's for an ice cream to eat on the way home?" Judy asked.

When she and Christopher arrived home it was difficult to tell who was more tired. She tucked him in and put a pot of tea on the stove. She would attempt to unwind and sort out the last few hours.

When the phone rang , she jumped. Phone calls lately were not harbingers of good things.

"Judy, is that you?" Alan asked.

"Yes, it is Alan," she replied, thrilled at the sound of his voice.

"If this isn't a good time, or you just don't want to talk to me at all, I'll understand," said Alan.

"No . . . no, it's a good time, and there was so much more I wanted to say tonight," she said, and before he could respond, she just let it all go.

When she had finished, Alan was heartbroken. He couldn't help think that her plight had much to do with his own inability to face his problems. He knew he had to do something to help her, but what?

"Dear Alan. The last thing I want to do is have any affect on your life and your relationship with your wife. I guess I just needed to let you know about Christopher and to have a shoulder to cry on. I feel better just having done that. I'll be alright now just knowing you are near," said Judy.

"Well, it's not going to be good enough for me, Judy. You changed my life tonight. Do you understand. You lifted me up from my miserable existence and gave my life a new meaning," said Alan.

"Oh, Alan. I've thought about you, missed you so much, and I wondered how you were," she cried.

"I had this overwhelming feeling that I let you down, and when I finally came to my senses in Mississippi, I was too embarrassed to call you or come home," replied Alan.

"Why in the world did you go to Mississippi," asked Judy.

"I have no idea, Judy, I think it's where I passed out for the final time. I slept in the car for a few weeks. One day while I was driving around feeling sorry for myself I came upon this driving range not to far from this huge shipyard. I was down to my last few dollars at the time. It was a stupid impulse, but I decided to hit a bucket of balls. I borrowed an old aluminum driver from the old guy running the place. You know . . . when I got through, I actually felt better. So I brought the empty bucket back to him and he said he thought I had a decent golf swing. Said I seemed to be favoring my right wrist thought.

"Hey, I'm not boring you with this, am I?" asked Alan.

"No dear, please continue."

"Anyway, I got to talking with him and he told me he was looking for some help at the range working behind the counter and driving the tractor with the ball rake on it. At that particular moment, it sure sounded good to me. As a matter of fact, I started the next day."

"The old guy's name was Russ, Russ Wheatly, and he was like a father to me during the next few weeks. Even rented me a little room he had out back."

"He always had a twinkle in his eye and a smile framed on his weather-beaten face that he displayed all day. Wore plaid knickers and a tam on his bald head like someone you might have seen on a golf course in Scotland a hundred years ago."

"He told me his son had been on the tour twenty years ago until a tragic automobile accident had claimed his life as he drove to a tournament. That same accident had injured his leg and caused him to walk with a cane. You should have seen the cane, Judy. He carved it out of a limb from a Southern Pine tree and varnished it hard as a rock. He was a master craftsman reconditioning old golf clubs, some of which adorn the fireplaces of a few of the finest club house tack rooms in the country."

"He sounds like a wonderful man, Alan, " said Judy.

" I guess I'll never forget him, Judy. After awhile he confessed that he had been following my exploits on the tour and he let me give lessons to his customers. Business really began to pick up, primarily from the shipyard workers who would stop in after their shifts. We stayed open until after midnight to accommodate them. Old Russ had to hire another helper when the demand for my lessons picked up."

"He was a real lover of the game and there wasn't anything he didn't know about golf. He could tell you how many times the U.S. Open had been played in Massachusetts or what Walter Hagen's favorite drink was. He would constantly remind me of how Ben Hogan came back from his crippling injuries and how I could also come back from my wrist injury."

"He eventually convinced me to come back here, come back and see a good osteopath. Well, I came back, but I never did see a doctor. I just didn't have the money and I guess I became content to just wallow in my own self pity," Alan said sadly.

"Well, maybe it's about time you did something about that wrist."

"I've been trying to put aside some money because I don't have any health insurance, but it's been like swimming upstream against a fast current.

Hey, enough of my dribble. I've already told you how much better I feel. Would you consider bringing Christopher to the shop tomorrow?" Alan asked.

"Oh, I don't think that would be an appropriate first meeting, Alan. We should be careful for his sake, and I have to pick my mother up from the hospital. Can you be a little patient, and I will call you," Judy replied as she heard the tea kettle singing on the stove.

"Judy, I want to help. Will you be thinking about how I can do that?" asked Alan.

"I will, Alan. I think I will sleep well for the first time in a long time tonight. Good night dear."

-MAKI

CHAPTER SIX

The parole hearing had gone well, and why shouldn't it. Bobby had been a model prisoner. The simple fact was, there just hadn't been much reformation needed in his case. He had simply been in the wrong place at the wrong time . . . wrong place, wrong time, wrong defense attorney. It had been a gross injustice and no one had cared. Something that occasionally happens in a free and democratic society, and he would live with it for the rest of his life.

Other than Carlos, Bobby hadn't told anyone on the outside of the exact day of his release, and he had decided not to call Alan until he had conducted some business.

There had been no inquiries from Steve Bronski. It was almost unnatural, and he carried an uneasiness as he was escorted through some of the last secured doors he vowed he would ever see again to pick up his few personal belongings.

During the last ten years he had forced himself to suppress the thought of his other personal belonging, the briefcase. Now he knew he would head right for it. Since Bronski had brought up the question of a cache, it had become an obsession. Could it possibly still be there? For that matter, was the building still there? Did he really need what was in the briefcase? A payback for the last decade? Not likely. What it really represented was closure, closure on a part of his life he would sooner forget.

It was a warm spring day in 1969 when he took his first few steps outside the prison. During his confinement President John Kennedy, Bobby Kennedy and Martin Luther King, Jr. had all been assassinated; the Cold War had gotten colder with the Cuban Missile Crisis; and the war was raging in Vietnam. It seemed as if the country had been an ill tasting stew in a cauldron of evil that he had been observing from an oddly secure, barred box.

Bobby's first few breaths of freedom tasted of pollens of trees starting to sprout again, fresh new flowers in front of the prison, and fresh mown grass. His sneezes attempted to break the mood, dramatically reminding him of his damned allergies.

He rounded the corner in front of the prison and walked along Commonwealth Avenue toward West Concord and the commuter rail station about a mile away.

The tall prison wall crowned with barbed wire ran parallel to the Avenue for several hundred yards and it felt ominous as he walked the sidewalk next to it.

He peered up at the guard tower and had the strange feeling he might be recognized and shot at mistakenly. Picking up his pace he finally reached the end of the wall where the residential neighborhood began. He was breathing hard and he had to slow down and remind himself, it was alright. He was really free.

There wouldn't be many happy memories of Concord Reformatory. In fact, he was lucky to be alive. Carlos had gotten several additional months tacked on to his sentence for physically tearing another convict off of Bobby's backside. That first year had been a living hell.

He would, however, remember the little surprise party some of his friends, and even a few of the guards had given him in the library. Release parties weren't that common, but he had eventually made many friends in prison.

There's something quite different about a friendship you make in prison, he thought. He now understood the real meaning of soul mate. It wasn't hard to empathize with many of the cons, but the others . . . you just stayed away from.

Bobby had told Carlos that he would hang around his home town of Hillston until his release day and then he'd be around to pick him up in his new Cadillac. They would then point it in a southerly direction and head for Miami.

"You are quite a dreamer, Mr. Bob. I cannot say it hasn't been fun, but could I trade the car for something with big teats and a soft pussy when we get there?" he had said jokingly.

"You had better, you horny bastard. Mary Fivefingers must have more than a few calluses by now," Bobby had replied as Carlos had completely broken up with laughter, laughter with an accent.

Bobby was reminded that Carlos was the other reason that he hoped that there might be something of worth in the briefcase to pay him back for his years of friendship.

It seemed like a long walk down the Avenue and along the way he even said good morning to a few people.

Man, would they be surprised is they knew they were saying good morning to an ex con, he thought, chuckling to himself.

Having almost reached the square, Bobby turned around to get another look at a particularly leggy young lady in a mini-skirt who had just passed him, and he saw something. A familiar figure driving a car a few hundred feet behind him. Had the morning sun not been at just the right angle, he probably would never have recognized him. Bobby turned around quickly so as not to appear suspicious.

That no good snooping bastard. I should have known why he took the pressure off me. He figured I'd head for the cache, if there was one. O.k. you son-of-a-bitch, lets have some fun, he thought as he continued walking.

He was finally in West Concord Square, and since it was nearly noon he'd find a place to have a bite to eat before he got on the train. Up ahead he spied a place called the Corna Restaurant directly across from the train station and he went in. The place was crowded with computer nerds from some of the new companies springing up in the area.

There was a long bar opposite the booth area and he was lucky to find a seat next to the door where he merely had to look into the mirror behind the bar to see anyone coming in.

A very attractive blond bartender in a low cut blouse was leaning over the bar wiping up. Bobby looked over just in time to see her soft, white breasts fall forward, accentuating her cleavage.

"What'll you have?" she asked as she looked over and made eye contact at an embarrassing moment.

Bobby had often joked about the lack of female sexual stimulation with Carlos many times, but at this particular moment, he knew he was also hurting. He quickly attempted to raise his field of vision to a Budweiser sign slightly over her shoulder.

"Oh, er... give me a bottle of Bud please," he replied.

She smiled as if to say, *nice try, but I don't mind.*

Almost in one motion she threw the bar rag behind the counter, grabbed a beer from the ice sink, opened it, and poured some of it into a glass before she set it down in front of him.

He didn't think he had ever seen anybody move so fast. Then again, living in prison on most days seemed almost like living in slow motion.

"How long do you have to work at this pace, Linda?" he asked reading the name tag pinned to her blouse.

"Well, I started my shift just before you came in, and I'll be here for eight hours today. It's busy right now, but it'll taper off for awhile until we get the late afternoon crowd. You want something to eat?" she asked.

"Yes, I would. For a long time now I've been dying for a nice big, juicy cheeseburger with french fries," he replied running his tongue over his lips.

"How would you like that done?" she asked him, having gotten the impression that it might have been awhile.

"Medium, please."

Linda wrote the order on a small slip of paper and then weaved her way past several other bartenders to a window at the other end of the bar.

Bobby was feeling more relaxed with every gulp as he enjoyed his new freedom, and his first beer in ten long years. The restaurant was obviously a very popular lunchtime retreat because people were pouring in.

He just happened to look up from his beer into the mirror behind the bar when his relaxed mood was broken by Bronski's ugly figure coming through the door. Upon sizing up Bobby's strategic position at the bar he apparently made a quick determination that he could either turn around and go back out the front door, or turn his back to Bobby and slither down to the other end of the crowded bar. He chose the later.

What neither Bobby or he had noticed was the dark complected man sitting six stools down from the door entrance.

Well, Mr. Asshole, I'm going to have a leisurely lunch and then you and I will take a little train ride into Beantown. I hope you don't have to work tonight.

When Linda returned with the burger he thought he'd ask her a question he already knew the answer to, just to stimulate some more conversation.

"Does that MBTA train I saw across the street go all the way to Boston?"

"I'm afraid I can't tell you that until you tell me your name," she replied coyly.

"Bobby . . . they call me Bobby," he replied with a smile, getting the distinct impression that she liked him a little, or then again, wondering if she treated all her customers with the same curiosity.

"I was baptized as Robert, but it always sounded kinda stuffy to me, so I prefer Bob or Bobby."

"Well, Bob or Bobby, that's a coincidence, my nephew's name is Robert, and the train does go to Boston. Would you like another beer to help wash that burger down?"

"Yes, I would, fair lady."

She set up the second beer with another smile and with the same speed she had served the first one.

"You've obviously been at this for awhile," he said as he glanced down at the end of the bar to see Bronski nursing a beer, with his large paw attempting to partially cover the side of his face.

"Well, I've been working part time in here for a few years now while I've been going to college. I got what you'd call a late start and my folks didn't have the money so I've been plugging along toward an Accounting degree at Framingham State," Linda said as she polished some beer mugs.

Bobby certainly wasn't drunk on the one beer he'd put away, but the combination of the drink, the food and the faint aroma of Linda's perfume whenever she came near was contributing to conflicting feelings of arousal and lethargy. It would be so easy to stay awhile, but Bronski's presence was breaking the mood and he knew what he had to do.

"Look, Linda. I have some business to attend to in Boston this afternoon. Will you still be here around six. I'd love to stop in and have supper and talk with you some more. If you don't mind, that is?"

"Can't refuse a paying customer," she said as she smiled and then responded to the little bell on the serving window shelf.

Bobby chased the last few french fries down with his beer, glanced down the bar at Bronski, and moved quickly out the door to the street.

The train to Boston was unusually crowded with young students who were obviously on a field trip to the big city. To say it was noisy with excitement and anticipation would have been an understatement. Teachers and parent volunteers were doing their best to convince the students that they must be in their seats before the train started.

MAKI

A smile pursed his lips as he thought of a similar field trip that one of his classes had taken on a bus to a Red Sox game many years ago. On the return trip he had bribed a classmate with a Tootsie Roll for a window seat that would eventually produce a painful ear ache for him.

Eventually the turmoil ceased and he was able to collect his thoughts. He knew where his ultimate destination would be, but it would be foolish to head directly for it.

It would be quite a hike from North Station and there was a lot of Beantown in between.

Remembering that Suffolk University was near the State House somewhere, he thought of how kind and sympathetic that his visiting professor had been in coming over to the prison to teach some law courses to him. *Yes, that would be a very appropriate place to stop along the way*, he thought.

When the train arrived at North Station Bobby looked back to catch a glimpse of Bronski in the car behind his just before the children jumped up from their seats. He proceeded out onto Causeway Street, looked down Canal Street, and instantly got another idea. Why not head down to old Scollay Square to see if the Old Howard and Casino Theaters were still there. He had spent more than a few hours there watching the likes of Blaze Starr and Tempest Storm while he was attending Northeastern. He remembered that he and his buddies would jump on a train at Park Station and ride one stop to that dark and forbidding station at Scollay. One did not go into that area alone at night. What a great place it would be to lead Bronski. He might even be able to get him engrossed in watching the strippers and eventually lose him.

When he reached the end of Canal Street, he couldn't believe what he saw. Scollay Square was gone and in its place was a huge, ultra modern building surrounded by other new buildings. It was a complex of some kind.

Good, God! he thought. *If this is what has become of Scollay Square, what does Park Square look like, and is the old Motor Mart Building still there?*

Well, Steve, it's too bad you're going to miss one of the highlights of our tour today.

He looked back to see Bronski duck into a store entrance.

Bobby turned up Sudbury Street and headed up toward the State House as he continued to look down at the maze of new structures just west of Fanueil Hall. He could see that the Union Oyster House was still there though. What a great place that would be to stop at on the way back.

Suffolk was located right behind the State House and he quickly located Professor Bingham's office. Luckily he was in, just between classes.

The Professor was gathering some books as he happened to glance into the anti-room past his secretary at the figure standing in the doorway. Sliding his bifocals down his long nose he paused for a moment to sort Bobby out of the thousands of students he had taught over the past thirty years.

"Well, I'll be. It's certainly good to see you in more pleasant surroundings, my boy," said the Professor as Bobby walked in past the perplexed, but smiling secretary.

"Just happened to be in the city and wanted to thank you again for all your encouragement and help," said Bobby extending his hand.

"It's been a great pleasure teaching you and the others at the prison, Bobby," said the Professor. "What do plan on doing with your degree?"

"I'm going to take a little while to sort some things out, sir, and I must still prepare for the bar exam where ever I decide to settle," said Bobby.

"Well, I certainly don't think you will have any trouble, and I hope you will include me as a reference on your resume," replied the Professor looking around for the glasses that were still on his nose.

MAKI

"Thank you, sir, that would really mean a lot to me. Thank you very much," said Bobby.

"Now, unfortunately I am a little late for my next class and I must run. I hope you will stop in again when we have a little more time to talk. You taught me a few things also, you know," said the exiting Professor. "By the way, based on your unpleasant experience with the courts, why don't you become a good defense attorney."

They both smiled at each other and Bobby reached out to shake his hand again, "I just might, sir. Thank you. I just might consider it."

As he descended the stairs to the street Bobby felt surprisingly energized by the conversation with his mentor. At the same time he wondered where Steve Bronski, Private Eye, had been waiting. When he hit the street he didn't see him, but he could sense that he was nearby.

He proceeded down Bowdoin to Beacon Street into the bustling tourists, students, business people and pan handlers. It was time to head for the old Statler Hotel and the Motor Mart Building. He would purposely avoid walking through the Common by proceeding down Beacon to Arlington Street.

He had used the Common as a short cut to the downtown area many times before but he had never really taken the time to drink in the beauty of its many variety of trees, its green open spaces dotted with gazebo's of various sizes and designs, and its flowers and wading pools.

Most of the trees had sprouted their leaves, except for the oaks who would begrudgingly show their broad greenery in another week or so, and be the last to shed them in the fall.

Why was it that I never took the time to appreciate this beautiful place in the heart of this city whose streets I walked while attending school? Could it be that the one positive thing I took from that stinking prison was a greater appreciation of life?

He was walking along Arlington Street in front of the Ritz-Carlton when the focus of his attention changed and he began to experience a slight sickness in the pit of his stomach. Was it the few beers he had for lunch? He thought not. It was more a sickness prompted by fear . . . fear spawned by his experiences that night ten years ago. He was approaching that part of the city that had been responsible for putting a young, promising college student in prison. He was reliving the experience as he walked along and he suddenly wanted to turn back, but he knew he couldn't. He had come too far. He must know if the parking garage where he had hidden the briefcase was still there. And yet, how could it be when half of the city had been demolished and rebuilt.

Bobby forced himself to continue, though the sickness hung in his gut like a meatball sub with too much of 'the works'. He carelessly crossed Boylston Street nearly getting hit by a zealous Boston cab driver.

One more block. God help me. One more block and I should know. There's the Statler. Yes . . . the hotel's still there. Now , a left on Shawmut.

Holding his stomach he looked back to see Bronski rounding the corner a few hundred feet behind him.

Oh, my god! There it is! It's still there..still there and apparently still being used as a garage. I don't believe it. he thought, trying to hide his excitement from Bronski who was close behind . *If there was one building in the city that should have been torn down for a more profitable structure, it should have been this one, and yet, parking was certainly at a premium in the Park Square area.*

Jesus, Bobby, take it easy now and just walk on by. Your main mission for today has been accomplished, he told himself.

He had an overwhelming compulsion to try and ditch Bronski and come back to see if the briefcase was still there, but it was too great a risk. He continued to walk along Shawmut to Stuart to Washington Street.

I've got to get rid of this prick anyway. He's not making me feel any better and he's testing my nerves.

71

Up on the right he spied the marquee to the PussyCat Cinema, a skin flick theater. Maybe that was the place to ditch him. He walked up to the ticket booth occupied by a sleazy looking character wearing a purple silk shirt and a narrow, yellow knit string tie stained with coffee. His dozen or so strands of greasy black hair looked to have been glued from one side of his nearly bald head to the other. He bought a ticket and walked in.

He was still feeling lousy, and now the sick feeling was mixing with anger. He didn't want to just lose Bronski. He wanted to teach him a lesson.

When he walked through the curtain from the lobby to the main theater it was darker than the inside of a sardine can and smelled just as bad. As he cautiously stepped forward his foot hit something on the floor and he bent over and picked up an empty glass Coke bottle.

The projectionist must have been fixing a broken splice in the film because suddenly the small crowd cheered as the film was restored just in time to show a well hung stud banging a cheap looking platinum blond, doggy style. Other than the screen, it was still pretty dark.

He stayed by the curtain up against the back wall, and ever so slowly his eyes began to adjust enough so he could discern some objects. Except for a group of sailors sitting near the front of the theater indicating their horny enthusiasm for the movie, another isolated individual who looked to have his situation well in hand and a few others sleeping off their perpetual hangovers, the theater was pretty vacant.

When Bronski came through the curtain he would experience the same night blindness, and Bobby would slip out.

He waited.

After what seemed like eternity, but was probably no more than a few minutes, Bronski walked through the curtain, but suddenly stopped, not moving more than a step from it.

Holy shit! I can't get by the son-of-a-bitch, and in another minute his eyes will adjust. I'll be dead meat standing here.

Bronski was so close he could smell him and he was sure if he took a breath he would surely turn toward him. He suddenly began to feel light headed from lack of air and panic enveloped him. Impulsively he raised the Coke bottle he had been holding and brought it down on Bronski's head just above the left temple.

Bronski let out a muffled grunt barely audible above the climax occurring on the screen. Amazingly he stayed on his feet for several seconds, almost as though nothing had happened, and then slowly began to slump.

Bobby quickly moved in front of him to support him before he hit the floor. Bronski was only a few inches taller than him, but he was built like a fireplug and Bobby moaned when his full weight came to bear on him. He quickly glanced over his shoulder at the patrons in the theater. No one had apparently seen it happen as he dragged Bronski into the back row, laid him down on the floor, and exited the theater onto Washington Street.

He flinched when he saw several MP's flipping their 'billys' coming towards him, and breathed a sigh of relief when they walked by.

He chastised himself as he rapidly walked along toward North Station.

You crazy bastard. You're just a few hours out of prison and you pull a stunt like this. Who am I kidding . . . that felt good. I just did something I've been dreaming about for years, he thought, smiling to himself.

He had put the Coke bottle back into his pocket. Pulling it out, he wiped it off and put it into a trash container on the sidewalk. There was really nothing to tie him to the assault.

Bronski might have a pretty good idea of who had done it when he awoke, but he could never be sure.

MAKI

* * *

He arrived back in West Concord around seven-thirty that evening and went straight to the Corna Restaurant. He was exhausted, and he needed someone to talk to. He was hoping Linda hadn't left yet.

When he sat down at the bar he was relieved to see her. She looked intent as she totaled up her receipts, but when she saw him she smiled.

Man, that smile was exactly what the doctor ordered, he thought.

"Well, you did come back after all. I was beginning to wonder," she said.

"Did you miss me?" Bobby asked playfully.

"I'm not sure, I was trying to understand why I should miss someone I don't really know. I was hoping you'd stop in again. Can I get you something?" she replied.

"Coffee . . . coffee would be just fine, thank you, Linda," he said looking into her eyes.

"You look tired. What have you been up to in Boston?" she asked bringing over a cup of coffee.

"You probably wouldn't believe me if I told you," he replied shaking his head.

"Are you hungry?" she asked.

"I think so, but I don't think I can eat right now. Look . . . Linda, there's more you should know about me. Would you mind very much if we went somewhere a little more private to talk? Maybe a coffee shop, or . . ."

"Bobby, I'm exhausted, and I really need to go back to my apartment and get some rest, but if you want to come up for a little while, I have a feeling I could trust you," she interrupted.

"Linda, you have no idea how much that would mean to me."

"Just give me about five minutes and I'll be ready," she said walking toward the kitchen.

Bobby kept a nervous eye at the front entrance. Would Bronski head back here after he awoke? Had he hit him too hard? Would the Boston police get involved? He only knew he wanted to get out of there as quickly as possible.

Linda's apartment was just three blocks away. She occupied the entire top floor of a two family house owned by her aunt.

"I was going to head for that Howard Johnson Motor Lodge down on Route 2," said Bobby as they entered her apartment. It was very modestly furnished, but neat as a pin. She directed him to the kitchen table covered with a pretty blue patterned oil cloth. A vase filled with spring flowers was set in the middle.

"You said you had something you wanted to talk about? Would you like something to eat or drink?" she asked.

Bobby began to feel uneasy as he looked around the room. He was very attracted to Linda, but this was too much of an imposition. He decided he would just spit it out, she would naturally be repelled, and he would leave.

"Thank you, Linda. You have been . . . a breath of spring, and much too kind, and . . . well . . . I must tell you that I was released from Concord Reformatory today. You see, I was involved in a situation that I didn't have much control over ten years ago, and it cost me a prison sentence. If you'd like me to leave, I'll understand," he said nervously shifting his feet.

Linda immediately sensed his sincere discomfort and honesty. "Look, I don't scare that easily. Please tell me more about it. I've suspected you felt some guilt about something since we first met."

Attempting to lessen the shock of his first revelation Bobby said, "About the only thing I came out of Concord with was a law degree. The rest was like a bad dream."

He found himself overcome with embarrassment. He stood up from the chair nervously parting his hair back with his fingers.

"Look, I can't tell you how much I've enjoyed your company, but . . . I think I'll head for a motel now. Maybe I'll . . . would it be alright if I stopped in tomorrow at the restaurant? If you're going to be working, that is. Before I get out of your life and head home. I'm so sorry about this . . . and I guess, about me."

"Nonsense! And don't feel you must tell me anymore tonight. I think we both could use some sleep. I want you to stay here tonight. Tomorrow you can tell me more, if you feel it necessary," she said firmly.

There were two huge bedrooms in the apartment, and Linda led Bobby to one of them.

"If you get hungry during the night, there's plenty of food in the refrigerator. Just help yourself. You won't bother me. I sleep like a rock," she said as she turned away.

Linda shut the door to the bedroom on her way out leaving her soft scent behind, and Bobby was alone for the first time in ten years.

He didn't quite know what to make of this unusually trusting and very attractive young woman, but he was too tired to think. Very quickly after he lay down, he was asleep.

CHAPTER SEVEN

A tall, dark haired woman walked into the visitor's room at Concord Reformatory, and every male head in the room turned. She was a classically beautiful Cuban. Her facial features were delicate and perfectly proportioned. Her exquisitely tailored peach colored suit complemented her creamy light brown skin. Her long legs seemed to go forever and finally disappear under her short skirt to somewhere fasten to her lovely hips. It was not difficult to imagine that her breasts were firm and ample.

She carried herself like a model and her piercing black eyes were fixed only upon the chair in which she would sit . . . sit and talk to a prisoner.

"Mi Carlos. Como esta usted," as her stoic expression immediately broke, and her eyes began to tear.

"I am fine, dear sister. Words cannot express how happy I am to see you," Carlos replied as he caught a wisp of the same delicate perfume his mother once wore . . . and it instantly reminded him of home.

They looked into each other's eyes without speaking for a moment, trying to remember the good times they had shared.

"Did you know that I am to be released in a few weeks?" he asked smiling.

"Yes, my dear brother, we have been counting the days. Our hearts have been heavy for you, she said fishing a small handkerchief from her purse.

"Echo de menos a mi familia, and you, Placida. You get more beautiful each time you visit. You should be married and making your husband happy instead of wasting your time with your useless brother."

"Oh, Carlos, there will be time, and besides, I have been offered a co-anchor position at one of Miami's major television stations."

"Holy Havana! My little sister is going to be a celebrity?" Carlos exclaimed so loudly that it caused everyone in the room to look over.

Placida blushed slightly, looked down at her folded hands and raised her head with a proud, broad smile framed by her beautiful lips.

"I am so glad that you will be able to share my happiness in Miami. You know that I am also very proud of you. You have endured more bad fortune and pain that several men experience in their lifetimes. You have worked hard to gain your engineering degree in this terrible place, and you are still a young man. You have many years of happiness and success ahead of you," she said.

"Leave it to my little sister to downplay her success. You never change my dear Placida. You could make the lowly cockroach soar like an eagle. Tell me, how are mother and father?" he asked excitedly.

"Mama prays for you each day. She has been happier lately. Her spirits are getting better as she awaits your return. It has been difficult for her, but she is in good health."

"And Papa?" he asked.

"Papa? God, you know your father, he has the energy of ten men. He has been maintaining a full medical practice and still finds time to meet with the committee to free Cuba. They have been trying to devise new ways to bring Castro down and to get more compatriots off of the island. He is hoping that you will also get involved."

"Yes, I would like that. I would like that very much. I feel much guilt that I have not suffered the pain of having to flee our homeland as most of you have. Yours has been a pain that goes to the heart and soul."

"Our hearts and souls are mending, as yours will slowly mend. It will take time," she replied. "Papa would also like to help you find a job. He knows many people in the Miami area, and he is well respected."

"If he doesn't mind, I would like to give it my best shot first. I know it will be difficult when they read my interesting resume. Oh, I see Mr. Almeda, you are a graduate of Concord Reformatory," he mimicked with a cynical smile.

"Don't be so hard on yourself, and try to take one day at a time my handsome brother. By the way, how is your good friend Bobby?" she asked.

"He was released just yesterday. I am worried about him. A certain guard here has been asking me questions, very personal questions about that night ten years ago. He has a very threatening nature. I don't trust him. I don't trust him at all. I'm afraid he is out to hurt Bobby," he replied somberly.

"The last time we spoke you told me that you were going to drive to Miami together," she asked.

Carlos's face brightened.

"Bobby says he is coming to pick me up in a big Cadillac on my release day," he said laughing.

"And just how does he plan to make enough money in a few weeks to pay for this big Cadillac?" she asked curiously.

"He says it may be an old second hand car, or a brand new one, depending on how things work out."

"How things work out? What things?"

Carlos's happy mood changed quickly to one of concern.

"I only wish I knew. That is one reason that I am worried. The other reason is this guard I told you about."

Placida looked at Carlos pensively, and then, in an assertive tone said, "Well, I think you should both get on a plane and fly down. I will even give you the money."

"Aha! Do I detect a hint of that same hot temper I seem to remember from a young girl in Havana?"

"It's just that I miss you so much, and now we will have to wait longer to see you," she replied with obvious concern for what Carlos had related to her.

" I am sorry, dear Placida, but Bobby and I have been compadres for a long time. He is coming to visit next week. Perhaps we can talk about it then," he replied.

"I do not think I will be able to see you again before you are released, so please take good care of yourself Carlos," she said dabbing her eyes with her handkerchief and returning it to her purse.

A guard began to approach Carlos. The visitation time had expired. He put his hand on Carlos's shoulder.

"That's it pal, " he said gruffly as his eyes fastened on to his lovely sister.

"Dios sea contigo, Carlos! We love you and will await your return," she said as he stumbled slightly upon rising from his chair.

"Give my best to everyone, and tell Mama not to worry. I will see you in a few weeks," Carlos replied looking over his shoulder.

* * *

Carlos and his family had lived in what would have been considered an upper middle class neighborhood near the Marianao beach front just a few miles west of the Almandares River in Cuba. The grand old city of Havana was virtually minutes away.

The lives and status of Cuba's professionals had changed little after March of 1952 when former president Fulgencio Batista decided to seize power once again.

However, Carlos remembered that his father's clientele had expanded somewhat to include some of the Americans who operated the gambling casinos.

He remembered the night his father received a call after midnight and was asked to report to one of the casino hotels to tend to an individual with an upset stomach. He didn't know until he got there that his patient was non other than the infamous alleged gangster Meyer Lansky.

His father was very surprised to see that Mr. Lansky wasn't at all like the gun wielding mobster portrayed in the movies. He appeared to be a very mild mannered, polite individual who was more concerned for his dog than he was for himself.

As much as Carlos had been told about that particular incident, he wasn't sure if his father was ever called to administer to Mr. Lansky again. He had been told by people who knew Lansky, that he was a very health conscious individual who drank very little and did no drugs whatsoever. He was a business man, and he often said that a business man must keep a clear head, and a keen eye. He could often be seen down on the casino floor amongst his table captains keeping that keen eye on the operation.

Carlos had decided to attend college in the United States for several reasons. Ever since Batista had assumed control in 1952 there seemed to be a constant air of political uncertainty, and the University of Havana was proving to be a hotbed of unrest.

Though he had not shared the same political views, he had known the young student Ruben Batista who had been shot taking part in a banned student demonstration memorializing Julio Antonio Mello who was one of Cuba's best known student leaders some thirty years earlier.

Additionally, the university was not particularly noted for its engineering curriculum, and Carlos had had his sights set on a career in engineering. Ironically, Castro would strengthen the science and engineering departments soon after he came to power.

Carlos's father had already sensed the unrest that existed in the country. There were young militants intent upon over-

MAKI

throwing the perceived corrupt government of Batista, and at the forefront was Fidel Castro and the Ortodoxo Youth Movement.

Both his father and mother wanted Carlos out of the country, and away from the controversy. Several of his father's cohorts had already sent their sons to Boston to be educated because it was known to many well to do Cubans as the American hub of knowledge.

Just at the time Carlos had been accepted to Northeastern University, young Fidel Castro and his brother Raoul were cooling their heels in prison as the result of their daring raid on the Moncado Barracks in Santiago. In spite of being sentenced to fifteen years in prison, young Fidel, who was actually an old man of twenty seven in 1953, was already perceived as somewhat of a hero. He would be released in 1955 as part of a political deal with Batista, and would head for Mexico to organize and train the army that would ultimately bring Batista down.

As he lay in his prison bunk, Carlos would often conjure up memories of the summer his family and his grandparents journeyed down to Santiago in their spacious 1948 Buick Roadmaster.

He and Placida sat in the back seat with Grandpapa playing games, enjoying the countryside, and occasionally getting into each other's hair.

It had seemed strange, but journeying to the other side of the island was almost like going to another country. It was the only time in his life that he would make the trip. Looking back on it, as he had so many times, he would never have known just how beautiful and majestic his homeland really was, had he not taken the trip.

There was only one major road that connected the extreme provinces of the island, and that road was over 600 miles long, just between Havana and Santiago.

At the time it seemed as though they would never reach their destination, but his more recent reflections were that it had served to bring the family closer together for those few weeks.

The highlight of the trip had been the little side trip to Guantanamo to see the mighty U. S. warships anchored in the bay.

He remembered the long return trip as being interrupted by frequent stops to add water to their car's overheated radiator. How nice it had been to finally return home to Marianao.

How could he have ever known, at that time, that the sweet memories of that trip would help to sustain him in prison.

Almost nightly, Carlos had regaled Bobby with stories of his adventures in Havana as a young boy, and when the lights went out he would replay them in his mind with his eyes closed, and than he would sleep.

His favorite places included the many beaches around the beautiful harbor, the magnificent Morro Castle, and the Castillo de la Real Fuerza, a fortified castle built to protect the populous against pirates centuries ago.

All of Havana was exciting for its many luxurious hotels, beautiful parks, and ornate old buildings, and his mind's eye he would stride over every cobblestone and brick to all of the destinations he had ever been. He would sip every former sight and structure like a rare wine to ward off the insanity . . . the insanity of his confinement, and the twisted souls of many of its inhabitants.

He had taken all of the letters his family had ever sent him to prison with him, and he would read them over and over again.

Sometime before that fateful night at the Latino Club his father would write:

MAKI

January 10, 1957

My Dear Carlos:

I hope that you are well and your studies are progressing without difficulty.

Your mother continues strong and as beautiful as ever. She and your headstrong sister Placida speak of you daily. Your grandmama and grandpapa are also well.

We appear to have passed safely into this new year, but I am apprehensive about the future. The storm clouds are gathering, and there is much concern in Havana. Concern of the rebellion taking place on the other side of the island.

Rumor is strong that Fidel Castro is gathering an army in the Sierra Meastra. He is said to have very able commandantes with the likes of his brother Raoul, Che Guevara, Juan Almeida, and Camilo Cienfuegos. I am sure that you have heard of these infidels.

Presidente Batista's informers say that Castro's forces currently number 200 men, and though not outwardly reflecting his concern, he will, necessarily need to be very alert.

I do not know how any armed insurrection will affect us here in Havana, but I do not want you to worry, because I will also remain vigilant. In any event, doctors will always be needed.

I will keep you informed, my dear son. Mama and Placida and myself wish you continued success in your studies and your good life.

Esta Vd. en lo mejor de la vida.

Love,
Papa

P.S. Mama is concerned that you are not taking well to the snow and cold, so she knitted this sweater for you.

CHAPTER EIGHT

It was several days later when the phone rang in the Pro Shop. Jeff was out giving a lesson, and Alan was working alone displaying some new golf shirts. Several customers browsed around, occasionally picking up a new club and giving it the traditional waggle.

"Hillston Municipal . . . Alan speaking."

"Hello, Alan?"

"Judy!" he replied exuberantly enough to cause a customer to casually look over. He lowered his voice while turning away.

"Judy . . . it's good to hear from you. I mean . . . I'm glad you called. I've been thinking about you and Christopher almost constantly during the last few days."

"Have you Alan? I'm glad. You sound so happy."

"Is everything o.k.? Did your mother get back from the hospital?" he asked.

"No. I'm going into Worcester tomorrow to pick her up. I talked to her last night and she's doing fine. Her cell count is up again, and they've adjusted her medications. Alan, I've been thinking about a more appropriate place for you to meet Christopher. I think the best place would be here, here at home."

One of the customers in the shop apparently decided he liked the last club he waggled, and wanted to hit a few balls with it across the street at the driving range. He pantomimed his intentions as Alan waved him over. Reaching behind the counter with the phone tucked under his chin he grabbed a roll of tape and applied a few strips to the club face.

"Hello, Alan, are you still there?"

"I'm sorry Judy, I was talking to a customer. I heard you, and I think you are absolutely right."

"Do you think you might be able to come over this afternoon? Christopher will be home from school around three o'clock."

"Oh boy. That's pretty short notice. I don't . . . wait a minute. Don't worry, I'll be there," Alan replied without vacillating further.

"Can you get here by 2:30. I'm pretty nervous about how to go about this . . . what to say to Christopher, that is. Maybe we could figure something out together."

"Sure, I know we can. I'm getting a little nervous here myself. Holy mackerel!"

Judy laughed. "I haven't heard you say that for a long time Alan. Where did you get that from?"

"I don't know. I guess . . . I guess I used to hear my dad say it. Funny thing is, I never used to like fish."

"I know. I remember. Lately I've been remembering more about you, and us. Trying to sort out the good from the not so good, do you know?"

"Yeah, I know . . . me too."

"Do you still think you can find my house?"

"Does a mackerel swim?" he said laughingly.

* * *

Judy and her family lived a fine old colonial house just off the Town Common in a quaint little New England village about ten miles south of Hillston. Pondville was originally a community of rolling farm land laced with brooks and streams which fed their clear waters to the region's many ponds and lakes.

It was also famous for its cookies. The old red brick building that housed the Pondville Cookie Company was still prominent in the business district. The town was currently more of a bedroom community for folks who worked as far east as Boston.

Alan had no trouble finding Judy's house. He could have found it blindfolded.

The grass needed cutting and the white picket fence was sorely in need of some fresh paint, but it was still the same old charming place.

God, she must really rattle around in this thing when her mother's away , he thought, *four huge bedrooms, it must be a little scary at night for her.*

As he unfastened the gate latch and proceeded to walk up the front walk he remembered how her father would always be the first one to great him at the door with a robust, "Good to see you young fellow!"

He wondered, if he were alive, how he might have been received by him today. Would he have been glad to see him?

Judy opened the door before he had a chance to ring the bell.

"Oh Alan, it's good to see you again," she said as she wrapped her arms around him.

She was wearing a white t-shirt tucked into a pair of washed jeans, and Alan felt a distant and familiar stirring. He could feel her firm breasts against his chest and his hands slid slowly from her back, to her waist, to her hips.

He had a tremendous compulsion to kiss her, but she broke the embrace by gently spinning out of it and taking him by the hand.

"Well what do you think of the old place," she asked as she made a panoramic gesture with her free arm.

"It looks exactly the same as I remember it," he replied, scanning the room.

"Oh . . . I should have known. A typical male reaction. Mother and I redecorated it after Daddy died. All except for his favorite chair. Mother wanted to keep it as a remembrance. You remember his old smoking chair, don't you?"

"Do I! I remember him digging out one of his old pipes one night for me to smoke. Boy, did I get sick. I think he was trying to teach me a lesson."

"Isn't that the night we went to Lake Shore Park and you got sick on the roller coaster?"

"I've got news for you," Alan said laughing, "I had a head start before we got there."

Suddenly remembering that they had little time Judy's brief, carefree mood abruptly changed. "Alan? . . . How are we going to do this?"

"Well . . . has he ever inquired about his Dad?"

"I told him his father went off to fight in Vietnam, and never came back."

"That's easy then. I'm back."

"Your back . . . just like that . . . your back? But not really. You're not back to stay. You can't be back to stay. Don't you understand?"

Judy began to cry. She made no attempt to hide her tears

He pulled her close, cradled her head in his hands, and kissed her tears. His arms encircled her and he kissed her mouth . . . her lovely mouth. His mind began swimming in the ecstasy of the moment.

"Judy . . . Judy. I was such a fool. Can you ever forgive me?" he asked pleadingly as he kissed her neck.

"I love you Alan. I always have, and I guess I always will. It was as much my fault. I was the one who abandoned you."

Just then, the sounds of excited school children exiting the school bus at the corner suddenly arrested their rekindled emotions. There would be no further time to embrace or to plan. Only time to absorb the tears, and hope that the meeting would go well.

"Hey, Mom! I'm home!" Christopher exclaimed as he burst through the front door.

He dropped his bookbag, and turned to see Judy and Alan standing in the living room.

"Christopher, I'd like you to meet someone." She hesitated. "I'd like you to meet . . . your father."

All of the energy and exuberance that had propelled Christopher through the day and ultimately through the front door seemed to dissipate for an instant as he quietly stared at the stranger standing by his mother.

"Huh? He's my dad? . . . But you said . . . You said my dad was lost in Vietnam. That's what I've been telling all my friends. Did he get captured? Where's his uniform? Say . . . have you been crying again, Mom?"

Alan resisted an urge to embrace his son. He knew in his heart that it might be a long time before it would be possible.

Judy took his hand, "Christopher, please come out to the kitchen where we can talk for a few minutes."

"But Mom, Gerald and I are going to play baseball. He's waiting for me."

"This is important, Christopher. He can wait," she said sternly.

They all sat down at the kitchen as Christopher suspiciously eyed the stranger introduced as his father.

Alan felt as though his heart would surely dissolve. He couldn't recall ever feeling so completely helpless, even after he broke his wrist.

This was a different kind of pain. Not a local pain, but a pain that swept through every tissue and bone in his body.

Christopher continued to stare at Alan.

"Are you really my dad, no foolin'?"

Alan smiled, "No foolin', Christopher. I'm your dad. My name is Alan."

"How come you're wearing a golf shirt?"

Alan hadn't realized it, but he was wearing a shirt with the golf course logo on it.

"Do you work at that golf course that Mom and I went to a few days ago?"

Alan was amazed at his son's perception. "Yes, Christopher, that was me that your mother came to meet that evening."

"Well, I bet I could hit a golf ball into one of those flag holes I saw there. I' m pretty good at sports, aren't I Mom?"

Judy was fighting back tears. It was the first conversation between Christopher and his father and Christopher was keeping him on his toes.

"How come when you got out of the war you went to work at that golf course, and didn't come home to see me and Mom?"

Alan nervously shifted his feet while Christopher searched his father's eyes for an answer.

"Someday, I'm going to do my best to explain why I did that. I just can't do it right now. Could I ask you to be patient with me until then?" Alan's voice was earnest.

"Well, I'm not sure I need a dad any more."

"Christopher Bergeron! That was a terrible thing to say. Apologize to your father."

"Judy . . . really . . . it's alright. I think I understand. Christopher needs time."

"Do you think it would be all right if I came over again at another time? Maybe we could go to a Red Sox game some day," Alan asked optimistically.

"Well, I guess so . . . if Mom comes too. Can I go out and play now Mom?"

"Yes you may dear. Please run up stairs and take off your school clothes first. Your jeans and sweatshirt are on your bed."

Christopher scampered up the stairs as Judy and Alan stood silently looking at each other. Judy broke the silence.

"Oh, Alan, I'm so sorry," she said.

"What's to be sorry about. That was a big first step, and we'll take some smaller ones. He's a fine boy, Judy. Time will tell if he can ever learn to trust and love me. I'll have to earn it."

Judy embraced him. "Thank you for coming over today."

Alan smiled and kissed her gently on the cheek.

"I have my work cut out for me, don't I?" he said as he walked down the front walk to his car.

She nodded as she silently attempted to assess what had taken place.

Driving back to the golf course Alan became acutely aware that he would have little time to reveal to Beth his previous relationship with Judy, not to mention the fact that he had a son.

He had little doubt that his revelation might destroy his marriage, a marriage already seriously strained. He felt sad that he and Beth had been drifting apart. It had been as much his fault as hers. There initial loneliness and passion for each other had been slowly replaced by their work. Or was it Beth's insistence not to want children while she was pursuing her career. He didn't know. He only knew he did not want to hurt her . . . but how could it not hurt.

*   *   *

Alan had always had a reasonable perception of his strengths and weaknesses. Many of those weaknesses were never so vivid as when he virtually destroyed himself attempting to compete with his injured wrist.

He knew from his experiences that he did not have the capacity to carry a hurt too long. He also knew that he would somehow have to tell Beth tonight and accept the consequences.

When he arrived home that evening he was exceptionally tired. The stress and anxiety associated with the events of the day had taken their toll.

MAKI

Beth was sitting at the kitchen table. Two orders of spaghetti and meatballs from a local fast food restaurant were on the counter.

"Would you like some wine, Alan?" she asked.

"Oh . . . sure, honey, some red wine sounds real good."

Spaghetti and meatballs were probably the last thing in the world he felt like eating. In fact, he wasn't the least bit hungry.

Beth filled two paper cups with wine and dumped the tepid contents of the boxes onto their plates, and they both sat silently picking away at their meals. She appeared to be particularly moody tonight as she quickly drank her first cup of wine and refilled it. Had she somehow found out. Maybe Jeff had dropped a little tidbit in her father's ear about the meeting with Judy last week.

"Beth, I have something I . . ."

It was if she hadn't heard his words at all. Suddenly, the thing she had been brooding about just gushed out like a trump card in a game of bridge.

"Alan . . . I have something to tell you!"

Oh, God , here it comes, he thought.

"I'm sorry to have to tell you like this, but I have met another man, and I love him."

Alan couldn't believe what he was hearing. Was she about to ask him for a divorce because she had met another man? He was stunned and instantly overcome with a strange mix of emotions. Her proclamation had completely negated his difficult confession, and yet, he found himself deeply hurt.

"You're sorry?" he said. "You are just sorry after nearly seven years of marriage? Who is this guy? Where did you meet him? How long have you two been seeing each other?"

"Please calm down Alan. He's a professor at the college. He's my Economics teacher. I don't know how it happened. It happened very innocently when he asked me out after class about six months ago. You don't know him. He's from Hopedale, and he doesn't play golf."

"So, this is why you have been coming in so late."

"Alan, you were always sleeping and he never came in the house. He has been a perfect gentleman and very concerned that this has happened during our marriage."

"I have a good mind to go and punch this guy out. I'll be the laughing stock of the golf course," Alan ranted as he suddenly found himself over dramatizing.

"Alan, I have already talked to Daddy, and he says that your job at the golf club will not be in jeopardy. I'm sure we can work out an equitable settlement. Please calm down. I'm sorry. I never meant to hurt you. Our relationship was dying long before I met him. I'm sure you would agree to that."

"So, where have you two been having your little rendezvous? At his place? He surer than hell hasn't been porking you at the local ice cream parlor."

"Alan, please don't make this any more difficult for me than it is. I'm sorry."

"Let me guess. This guy has a PHD, I'll bet."

"Well, it just doesn't matter, but he does have a PHD in Economics."

"Just as I thought, Piled Higher and Deeper. You always did like those highly educated types. How did you ever lower yourself to marry me?"

It was at this point that Beth started to cry and he knew he had gone too far . . . much too far with his performance. She really didn't deserve any more of his needless bullshit. She had no more wanted to hurt him, then he wanted to hurt her. Other than sexually they had simply not been compatible, perhaps from the very beginning.

"I'm sorry, Beth. I'm over reacting. I guess . . . I guess it's just because I'm hurt, and maybe I knew it was coming."

"Alan , you've gotten stronger since we were married, I've seen it. Someday you'll compete again and regain the success you deserve."

MAKI

Alan felt like a jerk. *That was a pretty magnanimous thing for her to say under the circumstances.*

"Beth, are you sure about this guy?"

"Yes, Alan, we are both very much in love and very compatible."

I'll bet they are, Alan thought.

"If you don't mind, Beth, I think I'd like to move out as soon as possible."

"Alan, there's really no need for that."

"I think I'd feel more comfortable."

"Where will you go?"

"I don't know right now. All I know is that I feel very tired and I'm going to bed. It's been a long day.

Little did she know just how long a day it had been, Alan thought as he walked back to their bedroom, grabbed his pillow and retreated to the spare bedroom.

"We can talk some more tomorrow, if you like, Alan," Beth yelled as he closed the bedroom door.

Alan closed his eyes and wondered just where he would go. He knew that asking Judy was out of the question.

What about the camp? Yes, that was a definite possibility. Other than a fireplace, it had no heat, but the days were getting warmer.

The camp was a three bedroom cottage that their grandfather had built on a pond a few miles outside of town. It had actually been used by everyone in the Makison family at one time or another. Alan and Bobby had probably used it more than anybody while growing up. It could be a perfect spot to stay while he worked things out, especially during the summer. It was actually the last piece of property the family owned. Tomorrow he would check it out.

CHAPTER NINE

He awoke in a mild panic, thrashing about. God it was bright. Where was the bunk bed over his head? Where was Carlos?

The sun was streaming in the window because he had been too tired to pull the shade. Blinding, warm sun . . . and what was that smell? Bacon cooking, and a hint of coffee.

I must have been back there for an instant, he thought. *How long will it take to forget?*

He rubbed his eyes, raised himself, and swung his legs over the side of the huge bed. As he looked around the room he felt as if he had been transported back to the turn of the century.

The furniture was very provincial looking, and there was an old porcelain wash bowl and pitcher on an ornate, mahogany bureau with shiny brass hardware in front of him. The floor was hardwood with delicate throw rugs scattered about. And lace . . . there was lace everywhere. It was a scene from 'Little Women'. If a stern looking old maid with her hair in a tight bun wearing a velvet dress with a cameo pin had walked in at that instant, she would not have been out of place.

As if by script, the door did open at that instant and the first thing he saw was a gleaming silver tray, not preceding a stern old maid, but a beautiful young woman. The tray carried the most delicious looking breakfast his eyes had ever feasted upon.

"I hope I'm not dreaming," he said rubbing his eyes again.

"I thought you might like something to eat, so I cooked up some eggs, bacon, toast and coffee. I hope orange juice is o.k.?" Linda said offering a glorious smile.

"What did I do to deserve this?" Bobby replied.

"Oh . . . lets just say you look deserving."

"I still can't believe you would invite a total stranger into your house to sleep for the night. I feel like saying you should be more careful, but then, I wouldn't be here, would I?"

"Well, I figured I could always call my Aunt Mabelle if you got unruly," Linda said looking at an oil painting at the opposite end of the room. "She's a black belt you know."

"Ah ha, she looks like a worthy opponent, but I have a black belt also . . . to hold up my pants."

"Whoops . . . I'd better be careful," Linda said laughing.

She was wearing a Boston Patriots sweatshirt and shorts. Her blond hair looked radiant in the sunlight, and he could now see that her eyes were light blue. Her lovely scent was beginning to mingle with the smell of breakfast. Under other circumstances she would have easily won the contest of aromas, but he was still puzzled by her unusual trust and caring, and he felt a strong sense of protectiveness for her. What was it about her vulnerability that could conjure up the tender feelings he had developed for her in such a short time?

"Have you eaten yet, Linda?"

"I was about to," she replied.

"I appreciate this very much, but I think I'd like to eat with you out in the kitchen. Just give me a minute to splash some water in my face and I'll join you."

She smiled and turned towards the kitchen as he quickly poured some water from the porcelain pitcher into the bowl, washed his face with a small hand towel left on the bureau and combed his hair.

I must tell her everything right from the beginning, he thought, *and if she doesn't understand, and I don't see why she should, I'll be on my way.*

At the kitchen table, Bobby launched into his life story between gulps of food and coffee.

Linda listened politely, but appeared to be less concerned listening, than Bobby was telling. She had already made up her mind about him. Call it woman's intuition or the inherited sense of looking into the soul of a person that her mother had passed on to her. She just knew that Bobby was a good man who had been thrust into one of life's unpredictable situations, and had reacted the only way he could have.

After his third cup of coffee, Bobby wiped his mouth and looked into Linda's eyes for the expression that he thought was inevitable.

"Well, in a nutshell, that's about it, up to this point in time, when I find myself sitting the table from Linda, the pretty and aspiring accountant who labors expertly as a waitress for her tuition."

Bobby had, however, left out the part about the briefcase. He hadn't quite known why. It hadn't seemed important in the telling. Maybe because the possibility existed that it was no longer there, or there was nothing of any value in it anyway. Perhaps because the situation had now gotten dangerous with Bronski stalking him, and he just couldn't implicate her.

Linda slid her hands across the table and took Bobby's hands in hers. He could now see that her expression was clearly one of compassion and caring.

"I hope you know, that in spite of all that has happened to you, you can move on and have a happy life," she said looking into his eyes.

His heart leaped and his eyes began to tear as he desperately tried to hold back his emotions. "I'd like to think so, but I think it will be awhile before I feel human again. I have memories to suppress and an institutional mentality tattooed on by brain."

Her hands felt so delicate and soft that if the table had not been between them at that instant, they surely would have embraced, and then . . .

No, he wouldn't allow himself to follow through with his desire. If this relationship was to mature, he wouldn't lead with his manliness. He slowly drew his hands back.

"Well, what's on your agenda for the day, Miss Linda?"

"Oh, I have a few classes this afternoon, and I have to work tonight from six to eleven. Doesn't that sound exciting?"

"More exciting than the existence I've lead for the past ten years," he said a bit sadly.

"I know, and I'm not complaining. I'm off tomorrow. Would you like to do something?

"Yes! That sounds great! Maybe there's something special you'd like to do? If not, we could ride out to my old home town. I've got to check in with a parole officer out there, and I could give you the grand tour of the furniture capitol of New England. You could even meet my famous brother Alan, the golf pro. Now ... doesn't that sound exciting?"

He and Linda laughed. He couldn't stop, it felt so good. How long had it been since his being had been cleansed with laughter, laughter with a caring young woman. A woman he was growing founder of by the hour.

"I guess it's settled then. You'll just have to stay another night," she said with a twinkle in her eye.

"Only if you let me buy some groceries to repay you," he replied.

"It's a deal. We'll go shopping this morning. Would you let me pick out some things for you at the clothing store?"

"Great! Oh, by the way, if anybody should ask about me at the restaurant, maybe it would be best if you didn't let on that you know me."

"Sure. Like I'm going to tell someone that you're staying with me. Is there something you haven't told me? Is there someone looking for you?"

"As a matter of fact, there might be. I'll tell you about it later, if you don't mind."

She seemed uneasy, but temporarily satisfied.

CHAPTER TEN

Alan was unusually light hearted at the golf course the next day. He wanted to call Judy and tell her the extraordinary news, but he knew she would be picking up her mother from the hospital.

He also knew that Beth's father would be in to see him. She would have called him again after she broke the news.

Sure enough, in about an hour he ambled into the pro shop and gestured for Alan to met him outside. He was very apologetic.

"Dammit! I would have bet that you two would be happy forever. You two had good chemistry. It's this damn era that we're living in. Half the young people in this world are divorced. Nobody respects the marriage vows anymore. I don't know what it's coming to."

Alan played along, listening politely. "I'm sorry Matt, I loved your daughter. There's not too much I can say. I'm really sorry it didn't work out."

"Look . . . I don't want you to worry, especially about the job. People will gab and get over it."

"Thanks Matt. I'm glad we'll still be friends. I only hope that Beth finds the happiness she's apparently been looking for, for quite awhile now."

Just then, one of Matt's foursome yelled over from the first tee. "Hey, Matt, get your ass over here. The group in front of us is on the green already."

"Look, we'll talk again, o.k.?" Matt said as he rushed over to the tee with his untied shoe laces dangling on the ground.

Alan felt a sense of relief walking back to the shop. *That wasn't too bad at all*, he thought. Now all he had to do was to find some time during the day to check out the camp.

When he entered the shop, Jeff motioned him over to the counter where a stocky uniformed man was waiting.

"What can I do . . . say, that's a nasty looking head injury you have there," Alan said looking at the large bandage above his temple.

"Yeah," he replied gruffly, "I whacked it on a door. You Bobby Makison's brother?"

Alan could see the Concord Reformatory emblem on his sleeve now.

"Yes, I am. Is he all right?"

"He got out the day before yesterday."

"He was released? Oh, my God . . . he did say it would be around this time, but he never called me."

"Then you haven't seen him?"

"No, I haven't, er . . . Mr . . . ? Now suppose you tell me what this is all about."

"The name is Bronski, Steve Bronski, and it's personal. He told me he might head back to his home town. I just wanted to see how he was making out."

Yeah, like a fox wants to find out how a rabbit's doing, Alan thought. It didn't take a genius to tell that by this man's demeanor that he really didn't give a rat's ass about Bobby's well being. This guy was downright mean looking.

"You wouldn't be holding out on me, Mister Fancy Dan golf pro?" barked Bronski.

"No, I wouldn't. Now I'd appreciate it if you'd kindly get out of here. I don't think I like your attitude, and I have work to do."

"O.k . . . o.k. I've got to head for work myself, but if you see him, tell him I'm looking to talk to him," said Bronski looking at his watch.

Bronski had managed to attract the attention of everyone in the shop, and all eyes followed him out the door.

"Man, that guy would be a perfect type cast for a movie, a very scary movie," said Jeff cautiously following Bronski's exit to his car in the parking lot.

"Well, he could be just a friend of my brother's. It may be nothing . . . nothing at all," doing his best to downplay the encounter.

"With friends like that guy I don't think your brother needs any enemies," Jeff said chuckling.

Alan went back to his chore of arranging the foursomes and tee times for tomorrows member guest tournament, but he was suddenly very concerned for Bobby's safety.

* * *

A few hours later Matt had made the turn with his foursome and walked into the clubhouse for a cold drink.

"Pro, I'm losing my shirt. I'm playing bogey golf, and my driving is killing me . . . I'm fading everything."

"I thought you might be getting yourself into trouble with that open stance I saw you using on the first tee," said Alan, "Try squaring yourself a little better at address, and move your right foot back an inch or two. See if that helps. You seem to be swinging outside-in."

"Thanks Pro! I owe you," Matt said chugging a fruit drink as he backed out the door.

"You don't owe me a thing," said Alan under his breath. "You don't owe me a damn thing."

Except for the encounter with Bronski that morning, Alan was in a happy mood. In fact, he couldn't remember when he had been so content.

Around eleven o'clock he had his head stuck under the counter when he heard a very poorly disguised voice.

"If your the Pro here, my lady and I would like to purchase a new set of 'Pings', complete with a bag and a fancy umbrella."

"Bobby! You son of a gun."

"How's it going big brother?"

Bobby was with a very attractive young lady.

"Well, aren't you going to introduce me to . . . No, this woman is obviously not with you.

I'm sorry, pretty lady, can I help you?" quipped Alan.

"OK, wise guy, this is my lady friend, Linda, and she's very anxious to meet my semi-famous brother."

"How do you do, Linda," Alan said with a smile. "I'll be damned, I thought you were going to call me, Bobby?"

Alan proceeded around the front of the counter to give each of then a hug.

"Damn, is it alright if I have seconds on that last hug with Linda?"

"No, as a matter of fact," Bobby said smiling, "Then you'd be one ahead of me."

"Oh?" Alan asked.

Bobby leveled his gaze at him and then, looking at Linda, "She and I just met. She'll be deciding if she wants to keep me or not."

"Well, if you decide to dump him, let me know."

"Hmm . . . I don't think Beth would like that," said Bobby.

"Beth and I are history, Bobby. We had it out last night. She wants a divorce."

"Ah, nuts, man. I'm sorry. Seems like the last time we talked everything was o.k.

"Well, to make a long story short, she's been seeing this professor at the college. But enough of that soap opera stuff." He stepped back. "Look at you . . . you look great. You both look great together."

Alan was being very careful not to allude to where Bobby had been for the last ten years.

"When and where did you both meet?" he asked looking at Linda who had been left out of the conversation until now.

"Actually, we met the same day Bobby was released. I work at the Corna Restaurant in West Concord and he just stopped in for a bite to eat," she said casting an affectionate glance at Bobby.

Alan appeared relieved.

"Well, I hope he kept his biting to the food," he said giving his brother a gentle punch in the arm. "Hey, this is a spur of the moment thing, but how would you guy's like to accompany me down to the camp? Now that I'm homeless again, I thought I might stay down there, for the summer anyway."

"Sure, that was going to be on our grand tour of the town anyway," said Bobby.

"Great! Let me find Jeff to cover for me. I'll even treat you two to lunch at Svenson's famous Scandinavian drive-in."

Walking out to the car, Alan grabbed Bobby's arm and whispered in his ear. "There was a prison guard in the shop this morning looking for you. Said his name was Bronski. Do you know him?"

"Dammit!" Bobby said, dropping back a few steps.

"You wouldn't have had anything to do with that bandage on his head, would you?"

"Yeah, I cold cocked him with a Coke bottle," said Bobby.

"Holy mackerel, Bobby, you what?" replied Alan as Linda began catching up to them.

Bobby grinned, "Alan, I almost forgot. You like mackerel too, don't you? I'll tell you about it later.

They all piled into the front seat of Alan's old Cadillac and proceeded to drive the five miles to the camp which was located on an L-shaped pond near the town line. Bobby and Alan were very quiet as they drove along.

"I sense you boys are reminiscing about the good old days at the camp?" Linda asked as she looked out the window at the gentle, rolling hills of central Massachusetts.

MAKI

"We had some good old days, and some bad old days down there. A lot of mixed emotions, right Bobby?"

Yeah, I try hard to remember Mom . . . when she wasn't sick, that is."

"What was her illness, Alan?" Linda asked.

"Her illness was alcoholism. I'd guess she started drinking heavily when she was around 35. She made it to the ripe old age of 42. It consumed her. She died a few days before my high school graduation. I had just visited her in the hospital the day before she died and couldn't erase the thought of all those tubes she had coming out of her. She was gone then.

I remember playing golf the next day . . . was on the old 5th hole when Bobby and Dad saw me and came over to tell me she had just died. I was so pissed off, I just kept playing. Didn't have much remorse left in me, just anger . . . so I just kept playing," said Alan, his voice dropping off.

"Why, Alan?" asked Linda.

"Why did I keep playing? I guess it didn't seem fair that alcohol should be able to capture the mind and body of a beautiful, intelligent and loving person. It still hurts to think that she never saw the results of the care and love she gave to us during our younger years," replied Alan.

"Hey, in my case, maybe it was a blessing," said Bobby.

"Bobby Makison! What a terrible thing to say. I'm sure she would have continued to love and support you through all of your difficulties, and I just know she is probably looking down from heaven right now just beaming with pride for both of you," said Linda assertively.

"I sure would like to think so," Bobby said, "I just wish the old man could have held it together instead of picking up where she left off. He missed a chunk of our lives, and he doesn't have beans to show for all the years he worked at a job he hated. Nothing but this broken down camp with no heat, no water, and a half moon outhouse on the side."

That little postscript even left Linda without a retort as they pulled off the main road at the drive-in theater.

"Hey, Bobby, did I ever tell you about the time some friends and myself rearranged the letters on that marquee back there. We spelled out..."

"Spare me that story again, please Alan," Bobby said. Their laughter helped break the dark mood.

When they arrived at the camp their grandfather had built, it seemed as if time had stood still. There were the two concrete and field stone pillars leaning slightly, but still standing on each side of the walk down to the beach. Bobby remembered that one of them was hollow and he used to hide toys in it when he was a youngster.

"Look at the old pavilion, Bobby, it's still standing. What a great place to fish from. Remember?"

Linda's eyes were bright. "This must have been a great place to grow up. I wish my folks could have had a camp like this. Can we go inside?"

They walked up the stairs to a large screen porch enclosed with rusted, torn screens, as Alan produced a key to the front door.

As they stepped in, the dry wood floors creaked loudly under the strain of the first intruders they had supported in years and they immediately picked up the familiar odor of half burned logs in the old stone fireplace blackened with soot.

They walked up the staircase to the second floor where three bedrooms and a little porch overlooked the lake. The mattresses on the beds smelled of mold and the curtains on the windows had yielded to the moths some time ago.

"Not bad ... not bad at all," said Alan looking around.

"Well, the old place could certainly use a woman's touch," Linda said shaking the dust off of an old bedspread.

"All this, and a short swim to the Polish Club for some weekend polka fun," Bobby said.

They walked out onto the porch, and Alan remembered what a great place it was on a warm summer day with the tall, slender white birches next to the camp providing a natural umbrella.

"Hey, Bobby? I'm afraid the old camp will have to do for the both of us if you still plan on coming home."

"Well, I will need a place to stay for a few weeks until Carlos is released," said Bobby as he looked over to Linda in time to see her bottom lip curl up slightly.

"I wish you'd plan on staying with me for a little while, Bobby. It's been nice having you around," she said.

"Linda, you've been awful nice to me, and I'd like that very much, but it would also be nice to spend some time back here in Hillston," Bobby replied.

"Ok, it's settled. When you do feel like coming home, you can stay down here with me," said Alan as he paused to hear a car drive slowly by the rear of the camp.

"Bobby, do you remember my old girl friend Judy?"

Bobby thought for a moment, "Wasn't she the pretty little girl from Pondville? Seems like when you weren't playing golf she was always on your arm."

"Well, it went a little beyond that. You see, we were very close to getting married when I was out on the tour. After I broke my wrist and started drinking, she left me . . . and rightly so. The thing is, I didn't know she was carrying our child when she left."

"Well, I'll be a monkey's uncle," Bobby exclaimed.

"Your an uncle, but he's not a monkey, he's a handsome young boy and his name is Christopher. I just met him."

"Oh, Alan, you must be thrilled," said Linda.

"I'm happy, but more than a little bit embarrassed with the way I conducted my life back then. I want to get back on track and patch things up with Judy."

"I have a strong feeling you will, Alan," said Bobby. "You sure have my support."

"That's great, Bobby," said Alan glancing at his watch, "Boy, I didn't realize what time it was. We'd better grab a bite to eat so I can get back before Jeff gives the shop away."

On the way out of the camp Linda noticed a rowboat that had been pulled out of the water and turned over.

"There's your transportation over to the Polish Club guys," said Linda.

"Ah, Ha, you've discovered another one of our grandfather's talents, boat building.

I don't think there was anything he couldn't build. I guess I'll have to get out the scraper, some sandpaper and a little paint so we can make it seaworthy again," Alan said running his hand over the keel.

"Wouldn't it be fun to invite Christopher and Judy down this weekend, and Linda and I could join you for a clean the camp party," said Bobby.

Alan's face lit up, "That's a great idea! Let me buy the hot dogs, hamburger, rolls and all that good stuff. I think the weather's supposed to be good. How about Sunday?"

"Sounds great to me. How about you, Linda?"

"If you promise you'll stay with me till then," she smiled.

As Alan pulled his car away from the camp he had the strangest feeling they were being watched, but he could see no one.

* * *

On the way back to West Concord that afternoon Bobby asked Linda if she wouldn't mind stopping by the State Hospital so he could visit his dad.

The Hillston State Hospital was one of a number of mental institutions throughout Massachusetts. It was located in East Hillston in rural farm country.

The complex had a remote semblance to that of a college campus except for the starkness of the many brick buildings with their barred windows. The buildings were as cold and impassioned as their contents, 'A' Building, 'B' Building, etc. The residents in the buildings had illnesses varying from alcoholism to manic depression.

For the less severe cases, and those who improved, there was work on the hospital farm or in the various supporting shops. Very small wages were even paid.

As they drove through the grounds very few patients could be seen outside the heavily secured buildings.

"If this place starts to get to you, just let me know, and we'll get the hell out of here," said Bobby looking around.

"I think if we follow the signs to the farm cottages we'll find the old man. Alan told me that's where they usually put him after he's dried out."

"Don't they segregate the patients based on the nature of their illnesses, Bobby? If I were an alcoholic and I was committed here just once, I don't think I'd touch another drop."

"I know what you mean, but the devil in the bottle always seems to keep luring him back, again and again. How many recovered drinkers do you know? Many of the old Scandinavians and Finns that I've known in this town who had the disease, eventually drank themselves to death."

They had passed through the campus area of the hospital and were coming up on large fields newly planted with corn and other vegetables. In the distance they could see the main farm building with several huge silos, and before it, a row of neat little cottages fronting a green. At the head of the green was a small administration building. Linda drove up and parked in one of several spots reserved for visitors and staff.

"Why don't you wait in the car and I'll go up and see if I can locate him. Lock the doors to be on the safe side," said Bobby with a wry smile. He scrambled up the stairs, and within a few seconds was back down.

"He's in the first cottage. We can leave the car here and walk over."

They knocked on the door of the cottage. There was no reply.

"Hello! Hello! Is there anyone here?" Bobby shouted. He turned the knob and pushed open the squeaky door. A lone figure was curled up in the fetal position on one of the cots at the far end of the room. Linda grabbed for Bobby's hand as they walked cautiously across the unusually stark room. There were few creature comforts. Bobby couldn't help but think that the cell he shared with Carlos was more appointed. You could sense that this was a place shared by lonely, forgotten men. There was probably little sociability here and even less caring for one another. It might possibly be worse than prison.

"Dad, is that you?" Bobby cried out.

The motionless figure seemed to stir slightly.

"Dad, it's your son, Bobby!"

The figure rolled over. "Bobby? My son Bobby?"

"Yes, Dad, it's me. How are you?"

In a voice that spoke much older than his 60 years, his father replied, "Oh, I'm o.k., I guess. Just a little tired."

Bobby's eyes began to well up. It was difficult to see his once strong, proud and intelligent father in such a setting. His reward for working for over 30 years, six days a week. Seeing his wife drink herself to death, losing his business, his home, and every cent he ever made. It was almost too painful to see this mere shell of a man lying before him.

His dad slowly rose to a sitting position, and could see more clearly that Bobby wasn't alone, but it didn't appear to register.

His hair was much too long and matted on the side that he had slept. His face told the story of a man tortured by life, heavily lined. His blue eyes swam in pools of red and he wore several days growth of beard.

"Have you come to bring me home to Hillston?" he pleaded.

Alan had told him that he always begged to be taken from the hospital, sometimes to the extent that he would get violent. But each time he had been released it would just be a matter of minutes before he headed to the nearest bar, only to start the cycle all over again. He was as hopeless an alcoholic as there was.

"Dad, I can't take you from the hospital yet. You must finish the treatment the doctors have planned for you."

"I can't stand the loneliness and the isolation here, Bobby. I think I'll go crazy first. Help me please. Help me!"

Linda could see that his father's pleading was tearing Bobby up inside. The old man was obviously still going through the prolonged withdrawal that accompanied his intense drinking binges. He had nothing on his mind but conning Bobby or anyone else in order to get that next drink.

"Bobby, do you think maybe we should let your dad get some more rest," replied Linda in an attempt to hasten the visit.

"Somebody told me that you were in prison, and I told him that he was lying. Not my son, I told him. No son of mine is in prison," his father shouted pointing his finger at Bobby.

How much more uncomfortable could this conversation get, thought Linda. "Bobby, do you mind if I wait in the car for you? I'm not feeling well," she asked.

"Oh, sure, Linda. I'm sorry. I think we'd best get moving."

"Sure, run out on your old man like you always have, and after all I've done for you.

That's what I get for bringing you into this world."

"Dad, I'm sorry we have to leave, but I'll be back. I promise," replied Bobby visibly shaken as he and Linda turned and proceeded to walk toward the door.

"That wasn't my dad, Linda. That wasn't the loving father I remember. You'll have to forgive him. Someday you'll see him as he really is."

They drove the long winding road from the hospital in silence. Linda wanted to stop just to hug Bobby, but she kept driving out to the highway that would head east , hopefully toward more sanity and serenity.

MAKI

CHAPTER ELEVEN

"Mother, it's go good to have you home again," said Judy as she placed her mother's walker alongside her easy chair.

"I can't tell you how happy I am to be out of that hospital Judith. I know I'm getting the best care in the world, and the doctors are wonderful, but it can be a lonely place. There's just too much time to think. Promise me, if things get worse, that you'll let me pass on here at home."

"Mother, I won't have you talking like that. You are going to get better, and that's that."

"Judith, dear, I know it's got to be hard for you to accept the facts, but I feel as though I'm losing this battle. They did another MRI and discovered the cancer has traveled up my spine. They discovered a small tumor in my skull, and they want to begin some radiation therapy."

"Oh, Mother. In addition to the chemotherapy?"

"Yes, I'm afraid so. Judith, I'm so tired, and the pain is getting worse. I just don't know if I want to do this anymore. Did you get the prescription for MS Contin filled? The doctor said I could take as much as I needed to be comfortable you know."

"I know Mother. Yes, I did get it filled and I'll get it for you. I want you to rest now, and then we'll talk some more. Can I put the TV on for you, your soaps are on."

"Yes, dear, that would be nice. I don't think I want to get in my bed just yet. Won't Christopher be home soon? I miss him so."

"He should be along any minute now, Mother. He's been asking about you. He misses you too."

"Can I make you some tea, Mother?" Judy asked as she headed for the kitchen.

"Thank you dear . . . Oh, I think I see the school bus."

It was only a moment before Christopher burst through the front door with what always seemed to Grandmother, energy to burn.

Oh, If she could only borrow just a tiny bit of that energy right now, she thought. She had always been so active, and now she was reduced to whiling away the hours doing the best she could to keep her spirits high for Judith and the boy. She had vowed that they must not see her despair.

"Hi Nanna! How are you feeling? Were you scared at the hospital? Your face looks a little puffy."

"I'm feeling fine, Christopher, just fine, and I wasn't afraid at the hospital. You shouldn't ever be afraid if you should have to go to the hospital. They are there to help you, and the doctors and nurses do the best they can to make you feel better. One of the ways they make me feel better is by giving me medicine. Some of that medicine makes my face a little puffy, that's all. Now tell me, what have you been up to young man?"

She already knew what he might say. Judy had told her about Alan on the way back from the hospital and her immediate feelings about it were mixed. She always knew that Judy still loved him, but his immature actions had been a source of conversations between her and Judy's father almost until the day he died. *If he were still alive*, she thought, *there would probably be no chance for reconciliation*.

Yet, she had always thought Alan to be a pleasant boy, very well mannered, and very goal oriented. She knew that, in spite of all his difficulties on the tour, he had never raised his hand to Judy or abused her. She would keep an open mind on the situation.

"Did Mom tell you that my dad came back?"

"Yes, she did Christopher. How do you feel about that?"

MAKI

"Well, o.k. I guess. It's kinda strange. Do you know what I mean, Nanna? Like . . . to have somebody come back after all these years and tell you he's your dad."

"I know exactly what you mean dear. We'll have to give it some time, won't we? We older folks have a saying that time heals all wounds."

"Well, that's just it, Nana. He came back from the Vietnam War, and he didn't have any wounds," Christopher said with a wrinkled brow.

"He certainly has some explaining to do, doesn't he Christopher? When you see him again you must listen very carefully to what he has to say, and try your very best to understand. Will you promise me that?"

"Yes, I will, Nanna. Do you know that I only have a few more weeks of school, and then I have a vacation? Boy, is that going to be fun. What are we going to do Mom? . . . for vacation I mean."

Judy had been observing the conversation between her mother and Christopher. It was obvious how much the boy meant in keeping her spirits high during her cancer treatment. Her mother loved him like he was her own, and was probably a big reason for her tolerant reaction to Alan's return.

"Honey, your mother doesn't have much money to go on an expensive vacation, but I promise we will take some day trips to some exciting places," Judy replied as she walked into the kitchen, put the tea pot on the stove and sat down at the kitchen table.

She would never admit it, not in front of her mother, but she was tired too. It probably had more to do with the excitement of having Alan back, but she had also been working for some time now at the local convenience store in the morning while Christopher was at school. She had wished that the job qualified her for a health plan, but at least she was able to be home by the time Christopher returned home from school in the afternoon. It was a precious time between a mother and her son, a time to listen, to offer advise, and to console, if necessary.

She closed her eyes for a few minutes while Christopher and his grandmother were talking in the living room. Her mind drifted back to those happy days when Alan was just starting on the tour, and they were traipsing around the country without a care, and not much more money.

The Los Angeles Open was the first tournament he had qualified to play in. She remembered that Alan had been a little nervous playing with the seed money put up by his sponsors. It had added to the pressure of having to perform well. However, for this tournament they had gotten a financial break by staying with an old school chum of hers who lived just a few miles away.

She remembered that the weather had been absolutely perfect, especially when one thought about what New Englanders were experiencing in January. Not too many people were braving the beaches, but with temperatures in the low seventies, it hadn't been too hard to take.

The tour kicked off in California every year with the likes of the Crosby tournament up at Pebble Beach and its sister courses. Bob Hope had his Desert Classic in Palm Springs, and Andy Williams had his tournament down in San Diego.

There were actually quite a few actors who were serious golfers, and they always made sure that their shooting schedules never interfered with the more important business at hand.

Hope and Crosby were probably the best known, but Andy played a decent game along with Burt Lancaster, Clint Eastwood, Phil Harris and Don Rickles. Needless to say, they were all better performers than golfers, but they added to the increasing popularity of the game.

As Judy continued to partially listen to Christopher relate his school work, she wondered where she had put the old autograph book that she had taken with her.

It contained the signatures of many of the celebrities who she had met that winter, including one from President Dwight D. Eisenhower who attended the Bob Hope Classic.

She had always had a strong sense of where Christopher had been conceived. She was sure it had been in San Diego. They had stayed at a nice motel just a few miles north of the city close to a beautiful beach. It had been a chilly evening by California standards when they had emerged from a restaurant near their motel, but the cool offshore breeze seemed to accentuate the refreshingly salty tinge to the air.

Judy remembered that the bottle of wine they had consumed while eating had relaxed then both, and she was feeling particularly amorous. Not seeing a soul on the beach, and very few young people roller-skating on the boardwalk, Alan had suggested they grab a few blankets from their car.

It had been one of several magic moments they had shared together, and as they walked further from the lights on the boardwalk toward the ocean, it almost appeared as though someone was turning up the rheostat for the stars.

They had spread the blankets near a large pyramidal shaped rock outcrop that looked as though some unseen force had pushed it up through the sand from below.

She could still remember the sound of the waves rolling in until they reached the shallows of the gently sloping beach to be slowed, broken and reduced to a foamy sheet of water that disappeared into the sand.

This is where they had made love, and this is where their precious son had been conceived. She had relived the memories of those tender moments a mere thousands of times.

"Hey Mom! Aren't you glad Nanna's home again? Boy, I sure am!" Christopher shouted as he emphatically released her from her peaceful daydream.

CHAPTER TWELVE

Carlos flinched, skinning his knuckles, as his screwdriver slipped off the head of a screw while assembling a bookcase.

Just another dumb lapse of concentration. Concentration made more difficult following each visit by Placida. Daydreams of life back on the island and happier times.

In his wildest dreams he could never have imagined a more satirical twist to his life. If only he had stayed in Cuba to attend college he might have been able to assist his family during their escape and would still be with them.

But what of his political views. Would he have continued to defend the highly questionable policies of Batista? He had often wondered.

He pulled out the drawer on his workbench and wriggled his left hand through a maze of nails, screws and other miscellaneous hardware attempting to find the small box of Band-Aids he had seen there.

"A little trouble there, my man?" echoed a deep voice from an adjoining workbench.

"I think I can handle it," said Carlos as he put his knuckle into his mouth to arrest the bleeding while he continued his search.

"Ahh . . . here they are."

"Now what you gonna do . . . now that you found 'em, put one on with one hand? Not likely, man . . . not likely. Get your ass and that Band-Aid box over here and let me help you," said the familiar voice.

"Good God almighty, I been watchin' you over there workin', and your head been like a thousand miles away.

Figured it was just a little more time before you done somethin' stupid."

"Well, Rodney, you were right, and only a few thousand miles off."

Rodney Brown, other wise known as 'Lip' Brown among the inmates was a lifer who had already served fifty years of a sentence imposed for accidentally killing a grocery store clerk in Mississippi over a bottle of pop when he was just nineteen years old. They called him 'Lip' because of his prominent hair lip which made it difficult for some people to understand him. He had never related exactly what had happened to anyone, except to say that he was grateful to the local Sheriff for rescuing him from an almost certain lynching by the local chapter of the KKK.

He was one of the patriarchs of the prison, a killer turned preacher, and a man respected by every con at Concord. Not much was known about his transfer from Mississippi State Prison some forty years ago.

"Here now . . . give me your hand," said Rodney as he removed the wrapper from a Band-Aid and tightened it around Carlos's knuckle.

He looked up at the graying old man, still remarkably fit and not really showing all of his seventy years. He was an otherwise handsome man who wore a moustache in an attempt to hide the extreme cleavage in his upper lip that the prison doctor had offered to repair many times for nothing. His reason for declining was always the same. "Ain't goin' nowhere anyway, but up there, where God don't care what a body look like."

"Hear tell you ain't got much more time to go," said Rodney. "How you feelin' 'bout dat?"

"Well . . . I am happy, but I am getting more nervous each day . . . and I am worried."

"What does a good man like you worry 'bout," asked Rodney as the supervising shop guard cast a curious glance over at the pair.

Carlos had learned to be very careful about what he said and who he said it to while in prison, but Rodney was one of very few men he had always felt he could trust.

"I have this very uneasy feeling that I cannot shake. I sense that there are people who know more of my concerns than I do," said Carlos turning his back to the curious guard and going through some simulated work movements.

"You wouldn't be talkin' 'bout Bronski now, would you?"

"Yes, how did you know?"

"Well, I seen how the man treat you."

"He seems to think I know something, something that will obviously be of benefit to him."

"Mr. Bronski has become involved in many shady deals while I have been here," said Rodney. "You should never be caught alone with the man. What do you think he be lookin' for?"

"I don't know, but it may involve something my friend Bobby has knowledge of."

"Somethin' that happened here?"

"I do not think so. Something to do with the crime we committed ten years ago."

"Knowin' Bronski like I do. It got to be involvin' money. He can smell it and he won't rest 'till he get it."

"I have been thinking that there might have been some money in the men's room that night, but Bobby never mentioned it to me."

"Your friend Bobby may also be in danger if he does know where this money is. Could he have found it at the scene and stashed it?"

"It is so bizarre. I saw no money. Why would he not tell me?"

"If he is a good friend like you say, maybe he didn't think you would be harmed if you knew nothing. If he is a bad friend maybe he will go to this money and you will never see him again."

MAKI

"No . . . no, he said he would return to pick me up . . . in a Cadillac. Holy mother!

I thought he was joking."

"You may have other things to think about, my man."

"What do you mean?"

"There must have been other people beside Mr. Bronski who were aware of money at the scene. It was about drugs, wasn't it?"

"Yes, how did you know?"

"I know it wasn't Girl Scout cookie money. I been away a long time, but that don't make me dumb."

"And you think these people could be out there, just waiting for Bobby and I?"

"I ain't sayin' they is anybody out there, but it be possible, Yeah . . . it be very possible. Man, it would be troublesome enough just figurin' out how to adjust out there without worryin' 'bout that possibility. I don't know if I could do it. I been cared for too long."

"Cared for? You call this being cared for? This is hell!" said Carlos, his voice rising.

"Hey, break it up over there! Cut the bullshit and get back to work!" bellowed the guard who had been watching them.

"See what I mean. Most days you don't even have to think at all, they does it for you," chuckled Rodney as he ambled back to his bench.

Carlos finished driving the final screw into the bookcase that would ultimately be put up for sale in the shop store. The conversation with Rodney hadn't been very reassuring and his insights would give him new cause for thought.

* * *

That night during the evening meal Carlos sought out a table in the mess hall with some of his Spanish speaking friends.

Amid the usual mixed greetings from the various Latin cons he sat down staring at a huge mound of semi-mashed potatoes that had been deposited very unceremoniously in the middle of some chipped beef on toast mixed with green peas.

"Hey, Carlos, where is your honky boyfriend," one of them gibed.

"Did you say honky or horny?" another returned.

"Mi amigo, give me a break, por favor. He was released a few days ago and I think he may be in danger. If I were not in this stinking rat hole I might be able to help him."

"Be careful what you say about this stinking rat hole, Carlos, the rats may be listening. Hey, no kidding bro'? Your pal Bobby sure helped a lot of guys in here with some good legal advice. Christ, I remember when my old lady was looking to get a divorce from me. I was Goddamned helpless, you know, like being in here and all. She sent her fucking lawyer here to intimidate the shit out of me, until I got some help from Bobby. He straightened that son-of-a-bitch out. What's his problem out there anyway? Donde?"

"Well, I don't know where he is, and you guys know as well as I do what got us in here. But what you may not know is that there may have been something in that bano . . . possibly some dinero."

"Quanto?"

"I don't know. I don't even know for sure what was in there, but I think Bobby knows, and he didn't want to tell me to protect me."

"Shit, man, is that why that bad ass Bronski has been on your fucking case? Cuidado, man!"

"Yes, but how can I be careful in this place of evil. I am at his mercy. He thinks I know something, and he is determined to get it."

"Well, that being the case, please allow us to keep an eye on you, amigo."

MAKI

"Si, gracias! I would be grateful . . . I would be very grateful," Carlos said with more confidence, managing a slight smile for his friends as he began to pick at his already cold meal.

CHAPTER THIRTEEN

It was the first semblance of a family get together in decades, though it was comprised of just two brothers. Two brothers from a broken family with vastly different life experiences. Two brothers and the women who loved them.

Judy had invited Christopher's friend Richard and judging by the shouts of excitement, they were having a good time. Alan had found some old inner tubes inside the camp, and they were doing a lot of bumping and splashing out on the lake.

The day was glorious. One of those rare days in late spring when the lows that like to ride the jet stream across the Northeast reluctantly give way to a radiantly sunny, warm high.

There were a few couples canoeing on the lake, and on the opposite shore people were starting to spread their blankets on the Polish Club beach. Later in the afternoon those same people would be consuming an occasional kielbasa with some kapusta and a beer or two.

Bobby was lying on the roof of the camp just off the back porch catching the warm sun and watching the children play. Occasionally his eyes would close, and he would try to remember some of his own childhood experiences at the camp. Then his mind would simply drift off, and he would catnap.

The serenity of the moment would only be interrupted by his obsessive desire to return to Boston, to determine once and for all, if the briefcase was still there.

Very slowly he began to formulate a plan, a plan that should be effective in getting him there in spite of being watched by Bronski. Taking a last look at the children he slid onto the porch and proceeded downstairs.

Judy and Linda had become fast friends. They were busy in the kitchen installing new shelving paper and rewashing some of the motley collection of dishes they had discovered. They were chattering away, making lady talk, and happy as a couple of sparrows at a new neighborhood bird feeder.

Bobby stuck his head in the kitchen door on the way by to ask if he could be of some help. He sensed what the answer would be.

"Thanks Honey, but this is woman's work," Linda replied, "Judy and I are having a ball. Can I get you a beer?"

"No thanks. I don't deserve one yet. Need to work up a sweat first," he said as he grabbed a rake on the front porch and headed down to talk to Alan who was raking the beach.

"Hey there bro, need some help?" he asked.

"Sure, join the fun. I think I do slightly better with a golf club, although I can think of a few shots I've had to make when this rake would have come in handy."

"Al, can I talk to you?" asked Bobby as he began to go through the motion of raking.

"If you can't talk to me, who can you talk to, little brother."

"Al, I'm about to tell you something that no one knows about but me. I was reluctant to tell you because there may be some danger involved."

"Does it have anything to do with that creep who was looking for you the other day?"

"Yes, it does."

Bobby began to slowly dredge up the incredible events of that evening ten years ago. They were almost too painful to recall. He told Alan everything, including how he hit Bronski in the theater.

Alan looked over his shoulder to the rear of the camp. "Holy shit, Bobby, do you think this guy is actually stalking you?"

"I'm afraid so, Al. Like a bird dog, and an ugly one at that. I'd be surprised if he's told anyone though. He's a greedy son-of-a-bitch."

"How are you going to get another look at that location again without him tailing you, Bobby?"

"Well, I got an idea when I was up on the roof just now, and I think it's a pretty low risk plan."

"How would you and Judy like to take in a show in Boston sometime soon? They tell me that new Playboy Club is very entertaining, and I can recommend a great place to park. Who knows, you might just have an extra passenger in your nice big trunk."

"Sure, I get it. He wouldn't have any reason to follow me, would he?"

"No Al, I really doubt it."

"Well, look at the two energetic workmen out here," said Judy as she and Linda came walking over to catch them leaning on their rakes.

"Looks like we came just in time, they look positively done in," replied Linda as she handed each of them a cold beer.

"Boy, I think we earned it, don't you Al?" said Bobby with a chuckle, and then he sneezed so loud the children even stopped playing and looked over. Everyone had a good laugh.

"Hey, who's hungry?" asked Bobby. They all replied affirmatively. "Great! Alan and I will get the grill going. You folks haven't tasted anything until you've tasted burgers and dogs cooked by the Makison brothers."

Bobby wasn't exactly sure of that last boisterous statement based on his obvious lack of experience during the last ten years, but he figured he and Alan could benefit from a little false confidence.

Alan got the fire going, and as Bobby was putting the hot dogs on the grill he had a flashback to Concord. Occasionally some of the cons would get their hands on something to cook out in the yard, but if you weren't part of their little clique, you merely watched.

He wondered how Carlos was holding up. It could be a jeopardous time for him. Everybody in the joint knew how much time everyone else had left to do, and there were hard timers and even some guards who would jump at the chance to screw a guy who was on the way out. He remembered trying to pick up Carlos's spirits by telling him that he would pick him up in a Cadillac, and he wondered now if he might have to settle for a cab.

Amazingly enough, the food cooked by the two cocky chefs was edible. The girls started to clean up, and Christopher and his friend went down to the lake for a final swim. Bobby grabbed Alan's arm and they quickly walked to the rear of the camp where Alan's car was parked.

"Let's give this trunk escape a little practice run," Bobby said, "I know you have a release lever, but I've got to make sure I can get out of this thing myself."

They both looked around to assure no one was observing and Alan opened his trunk, lifted his golf clubs out, and Bobby climbed in with screwdriver and a flashlight he had found in the glove compartment.

"O.k., close her down."

After a few minutes of finding out where to apply leverage to the locking mechanism, the lid popped open and Bobby sat there smiling. "The great Houdini does it again."

"My little brother, the James Bond of Hillston. I think it should work just fine, Bobby, and this way we don't have to worry Judy at all."

They hustled back to the front of the camp to find that the girls had just finished cleaning up.

"There they are," replied Linda, "What have you two boys been up to?"

"Damn, we're sorry," said Alan, "I was just showing Bobby my golf clubs."

"I see . . . how very convenient," answered Judy with a subtle smile. "We left the grill for you to clean."

"Yes, ma'am! Let's do it , Bobby."

Judy looked toward the lake and shouted, "Christopher! Richard! You boys better get out of the water now and get changed up. Alan's going to drive us home and then he's coming back to sleep at the camp with Bobby and Linda."

* * *

As Alan drove toward Pondvale that evening his mind seemed to be working overtime. It had been a very relaxing day, relaxing until Bobby's revelation, that is. What would come of this sojourn to Boston? Could there possibly be anything of value in this briefcase he spoke of? His thought process was interrupted when Judy asked, "Did you boys have fun today?"

"Boy! Did we! Could we go back again?" asked Christopher.

"You guys are welcome back again as far as I'm concerned. Maybe Bobby and I can get working on that boat so we can do a little fishing, and . . . by the way . . . you boys could use a little swimming instruction. You can't spend all of your time floating around on those tubes. You've got to learn how to take care of yourself in the water. Next time, I'll give you both a swimming lesson to start the day, and then you'll have something to work on when you get tired of those tubes."

"Then can we go fishing, Dad?"

Alan paused just long enough to savor being called Dad. It was really the first time Christopher had used the acknowledgement. He looked over at Judy. She was smiling from ear to ear. She had also been wondering when his son would warm enough to address him properly.

MAKI

"You bet we can. I'll take you over to some guaranteed fishing spots. Why, some day I might tell you about the two hour battle I had out there with this giant pickerel. It was a foggy morning, and . . ."

"Alan, honey. Why don't you save that fish story for another day, Richard's house is right around the corner and I'm sure he'd want to hear the entire exciting story."

"Oh, yeah, sure," Alan said laughing, and the entire car joined in.

After they dropped Richard off, Judy asked Alan if he'd like to come in and say hello to Vera.

"She always liked you very much, and I know she'd like to talk to you for a few minutes."

"I'd like that," said Alan with mixed feelings, wondering what she really might say. He knew that if he were to ever make things right with Judy and Christopher, he would need to confront her mother. He sensed that his chances of regaining her confidence might be good, not just because he knew that she cared about him, but because he also cared for her and was anxious to offer his compassion and any assistance he could.

Christopher set a good tone as he bounded into the house with all the news of the day.

"Nana! Nana! Richard and I swam all day, and played on the beach, and we had hot dogs and hamburgers, and . . ."

"Hold on, honey. You've got to slow down for your grandmother," Judy interrupted.

"Mother, there's someone here who would like to say hello."

"Oh, my goodness. Alan! You really haven't changed much. How have you been?"

"I'm fine, Mrs. Bergeron, and thanks for not mentioning my receding hairline."

"I think it's wonderful that you will be seeing more of my daughter and Christopher."

"I'd like to see more of you also, Mrs. Bergeron. I want you to know that you can depend on me from now on," Alan said.

"Then I guess you'd better start be being a little less formal and calling me Vera."

"Thank you, Vera, and how have you been feeling? I understand you have a battle on your hands."

"Christopher, would you run upstairs and run some bath water for yourself, please.

Then you can come back down and tell Nanna all of the news, and, by the way, thanks for being such a good boy today."

"O.k. Mom." Christopher scampered up the stairs, got to the top, and leaned back with his nose between the balusters.

"When will I see you again, Dad?"

"I'll see you tomorrow, if it's alright with your mom," replied Alan looking toward Judy.

"That's great, Dad!" Christopher exulted as he continued on up the stairs.

"Don't forget to use the soap, young man," Judy shouted smiling broadly.

"He's quite a boy, isn't he?" said Alan.

"Yes, he's all boy," Vera spoke up. "Alan, would you like to stay for awhile?"

Alan sensed that they were all a little tired and thought it best to ease himself out.

"Thank you Vera, but it's getting late, and I really should be leaving. May I stop by tomorrow and see you?"

"I wish you would dear," she said.

Alan walked with Judy back to the foyer. Her hand felt good in his, and he looked forward to her embrace before he left. When they were out of sight of her mother, he put his arms around her, and a hug quickly became a passionate kiss.

"I had a wonderful day, Alan. We were almost like family, weren't we?"

"Yes . . . almost. I feel good about this, Judy. I feel good about you again, and knowing I have a son has given me a new sense of myself."

"I'm glad, Alan. I wondered if I was doing the right thing by calling you."

"Nothing could have been so right," replied Alan.

CHAPTER FOURTEEN

Everything went like clockwork. Bobby slipped into Alan's car trunk while they were at the camp and he proceeded to pick up Judy in Pondvale for their trip to the Playboy Club in Boston.

Bobby had been reasonably certain that Bronski would be at the prison for another hour, but the plan should assure that no one would know where he had gone except for Alan. He had covered himself with Linda by telling her that he had a appointment with his probation officer late that afternoon.

It was warm by the time they left and before long the heat in the trunk became almost unbearable, something Bobby hadn't counted on. He tried to remain as motionless as possible on the way into Boston, but found that he frequently had to shift positions to avoid stiffening up. He chastised himself as the sweat began to soak his shirt and his back began to hurt. Why hadn't he thought to take along one of the air mattresses at the camp.

A long hour and a half later Bobby finally felt the car making hard turns and accelerating up the steep ramps in the Motor Mart Garage. His heart was pounding furiously with anxiety.

He had told Alan approximately where to park on the third floor. He sensed that Alan must have been successful in finding a spot because the car was backing up, and then it came to a stop.

Alan had arranged to meet another golfing buddy and his wife at the club, just across the street from the Common. In addition to having supper and seeing a show they were also going to see if they could play in the Playboy Club's annual golf tournament at Pleasant Valley Country Club.

He heard Alan say, "They tell me the shows are pretty good at the club, honey, and the food is excellent."

"Yeah, right," quipped Judy, "I'm sure you're not even going to notice the Bunnies, Alan?"

"Oh? They have Bunnies?" Alan joked, and Bobby could hear them laughing as they walked toward the stairwell. The Playboy Club was only a block away.

Bobby waited until it was quiet, except for the drone of an occasional automobile going up the ramps. When all noise had subsided, he popped the trunk open with his screwdriver. His only other tool was a Swiss Army knife he had purchased. If the briefcase was still there, he thought he might be able to pick the lock, or at the very least cut the strap that fastened it to the locking mechanism.

Alan had backed the car up to within a few feet of the outer wall, leaving room for Bobby to slip out, conceal himself, and assess the situation before proceeding. The parking space was right next to the stairwell Bobby had described. Now . . . was this the same location where he had hidden the briefcase?

He moved slowly in back of the well and, just as he had ten years ago, began climbing the steel window frame. It was slippery because of the dust and dirt that had accumulated over the years. When he got to a point he could support himself adequately, he looked up.

There was something up there alright, and it surer than hell looked liked it could be the briefcase, crammed up in a recess just about where it should be. It was barely distinguishable because of the heavy coating of automobile emission soot.

Ten years, he thought. For ten years this is the moment I thought about. The crazy idea that it might still be here and there might be something in it to justify wasting that much time at Concord. Know-ing that for the rest of my life I would be labeled an ex-con.

His emotions gave way to a flood of tears, almost causing him to lose his grip. *Wait a minute you damn fool. Your finally here, and it's here . . . don't blow it now.*

A few more cautious steps along the frame . . . a tug . . . and it came loose, dropping and hitting him flush in the face. He was stunned by the impact, nearly blinded by the soot, and almost lost his balance again. It fell to the floor with a thud.

Wiping the dust out of his eyes with his forearm, he stead-ied his footing, and slowly inched his way down. He grabbed the briefcase at about the same time the door to the stairwell opened.

The young couple who emerged apparently hadn't had much to say to each other on the way up, because there had been no warning of their approach. Bobby clutched the case to his chest and pressed hard against the stairwell so as not to be seen.

He took a breath, held it, and listened. Their footsteps ap-peared to fade away. A car door slammed . . . and then another. They were gone. Thank God they hadn't come up a few sec-onds earlier. It wasn't so much that he couldn't make up some kind of story, he just didn't want to be seen, by anyone.

He couldn't recall the briefcase being so heavy. Why? Had the leather become so moisture laden? Had his adrena-line laced fear that night ten years ago made it feel lighter?

He ducked down and made his way back to the car. He wanted to open the case, but he dared not do it outside the safe confines of the trunk. The sound of two men arguing on the same floor some distance away caused him to stop mo-mentarily.

Quickly, he slipped back into the trunk, located his flash-light, and closed the lid very carefully until the locking mecha-nism clicked close.

MAKI

The smell of must emanating from the briefcase was over-powering as he reached into his pocket for his jackknife. He fumbled to open it only to see several drops of blood splatter onto the blade. He had been so completely consumed with his objective he hadn't noticed that the falling briefcase had opened a small cut across the bridge of his nose. Drawing out his handkerchief, he applied pressure to the cut.

Looking at the lock he could see that picking it would be very difficult, so he began sawing across the strap. It was a tedious process. He began to wonder how much time had elapsed. It seemed like hours, but couldn't have been more than fifteen minutes. His nose began bleeding again. The frustration and anxiety were taking their toll.

Half way through! Yes, it was doable. Three quarters through. His hand hurt. *Just a little more . . . there!*

He flipped the top of the briefcase back and shined the light in it. *Oh no, what's this . . . newspaper? Yes, but something else. Packages . . . packages of bills, under the newspaper.* Apparently the paper had been stuffed on top. Underneath were packages of twenties, fifties and hundred dollar bills.

His heart was pounding furiously. Someone would surely hear it, he thought. How much money was in it? He had no idea. He had never seen so much money. He wanted to scream with ecstasy. No, he couldn't, he must suppress his desire to shout. He must wait.

Well, at least he would have something to do while waiting for Alan to return . . . count money. He began to with-draw the packages and arrange them in piles. There were apparently one hundred bills in each package. He tried to stack them ten high. They kept falling over. He became giddy as he fanned each package before laying them down. Maybe he'd better wait, when he was more composed, when he had more room. No, he had to know. He had to know what ten years in prison had been worth . . . what each lousy, oppressive day had been worth.

Just then, he thought he heard something. Probably just someone else returning from a local club or a movie. No, it was the same voices he had heard a short time ago, the men who had been arguing. He stopped counting and shut off his flashlight in case there was a chance the light might be seen through one of the trunk gaskets. The stairwell door opened and closed.

"You just have no taste, my man. You can't help it, always doin' those Saabs and Volvo's and the like. You are one sorry motherfucker. Now you take this fine automobile, this classic American work of art. This is truly worthy of my infinite skill," said one of the voices.

"Shit, man . . . you jivin' me? Is that what you doin'? I ain't wasting my good time on this old relic of a Cadillac. If you want to do it, be my guest, but I am not seatin' my sorry ass in that motherfucking piece of metal," replied the second voice as it proceeded further down the aisle.

"Well now, let us just see, how good I can be. I may just ride this honey south to my Providence Paisano's."

Bobby heard the scrape of something being forced through the window molding, then he heard the click of the door lock. It was all too clear what was happening. The door opened, and a few moments later, the engine started. He was going for an unscheduled ride.

He couldn't believe it. Everything had gone so smooth. How in God's name could he have anticipated Alan's car being stolen? Was that guy kidding? Was he headed for Providence?

The car was flying down the ramps. He thought about jumping out, but he couldn't risk it. If he didn't injure himself, he'd surely be seen. How would this guy get past the toll taker? If Alan had left the ticket in the car, all he had to do was pay the amount due. What would look more natural than a black guy in a Caddy. He heard the gate buzz on the bottom floor, and they were off.

He knew it was only a few minutes to the Southeast Expressway, then an easy drive south to pick up Route 128 to 95. Then, on to Providence, it that's where he was headed.

His chauffeur turned on a rhythm and blues station and cranked up the volume. He thought his eardrums would burst in the trunk where the speakers were located. He began gathering up the money and throwing it back into the briefcase. The moldy smell was triggering his allergies and he felt a sneeze coming on. He couldn't suppress it.

"Aaah . . . chu!"

The driver must have thought he heard something, because he turned the volume down to a whisper. Bobby wondered if he might have a gun. Surely he must have a knife. He held his breath. Would the driver stop? Seconds that seemed like minutes passed. The driver turned up the volume again.

He slowly reached around for his handkerchief and held it over his nose to try and filter out what was causing the problem.

An hour passed. The car began to slow down. It stopped. The driver's side door opened and closed. Could he risk jumping out now? He'd need to carry the heavy briefcase under his arm because the strap was severed. He'd wait a few minutes first.

Voices approaching!

"Hey Goombah, look what the shine brought us, a fucking stud-mobile."

"Fuck me, man. What the fuck are we gonna do wit dis? Huh, shit head? Jesus Christ, Sambo, did you honestly think you could dump this nigger van wit us? You betta keep it for yourself."

"You must be jivin me, my man. I been driving half the fucking night to deliver this pearl to you all."

"Well, shit man, I can't chop it, and I can't sell it, especially ta doze fancy Brown University fucks on da hill. De'r into them foreign jobbers, you dig?"

"If I take this motherfucker back to Beantown, it's just gonna be too fucking hot."

"Well, my guinea heart is breakin' for your black ass. I'll give ya two small ones for it."

"Shit, man, you is pullin my chain big time. That ain't barely cab fare home."

Bobby sensed that tempers were beginning to stretch beyond their breaking points.

"Don't gimme that crap. You can score another set a wheels here in town. Take it, or leave it. Me an Tony gotta get back to da club."

Bobby could hear the driver muttering to himself, and it sounded like he had turned away. He apparently had no intention of taking a hit on the car he had grown very attached to during the drive down.

"Well then. You two fine Italian gents leave me no alternative then to take this priceless piece of transportation back to show my woman."

"I don't give a fuck what you do, jus get dis piece o shit and your black ass off the fuckin' hill."

"Hey Vito . . . Vito, we cannot treat our valued transporter too shabby, else he may not want to do any future business. How bout I cough up another bill. What do ya say, huh?"

"No way, man. I need five for this lovely mobile, and that's final."

"Final?!! I'll give you a fuckin' final," as the man called Vito struggled to draw what looked to be a piece from his shoulder holster.

The black man dove behind the wheel, started the car and was off before the gun cleared the holster. The acceleration was so severe it caused Bobby to slide abruptly to the rear of the trunk. At the same time he heard a shot ring out from behind him, and was very happy that the projectile did not enter the trunk. This Vito character was either firing for effect, or was just a bad shot. Regardless, Bobby was grateful not to have to quell any further bleeding on his posterior and was obviously heading back to Boston.

The driver didn't waste any time turning on his favorite radio station for the short ride North, and this time it didn't sound bad at all . . . no sir, not bad at all.

* * *

He must have dozed off, because the slamming of the car door scared him awake. He suddenly developed an overwhelming feeling of claustrophobia. It was the same feeling he used to get in prison. It had taken him months to get over being confined in a cell. He would lie in his bunk and feel the cold sweats start. There was no way he could stop them. When he became totally drenched, they would pass. He knew he had to get out of the trunk.

The driver had apparently gone into a residence nearby. He had to chance it. He popped open the trunk release and raised the trunk lid only enough to see out. He was on a side street . . . on a hill somewhere . . . but where? He wasn't aware of any hill in Boston other than Beacon Hill. The fact was, he didn't know too much about Boston other than the Back Bay.

He carefully raised the trunk lid and slid out serpent like, with the briefcase under his arm, pausing in a squatting position between the parked cars.

Now what? Got to get to a phone, but where do you find a phone at 2 A.M.? Maybe look for a cop in a cruiser. Yeah, that would be smart. Imagine trying to explain about the money.

Someone was coming. He hunkered down lower. Just a drunk clutching what was once a full bottle of wine in a bag. He kept putting it up to his mouth like there was still something left in it, and then, realizing it was empty, threw it right where Bobby was. The bottle ricocheted off his shoulder and sent a sharp pain down his arm. He bit his lip to squelch a scream. The drunk had never seen him, much less anything else.

Bobby rose up, trying to massage his shoulder and hold on to the briefcase at the same time. The drunk had been a black man. Was that a clue to where he was? A sign ahead on the corner read Calumet Street and St. Alphonsus. He headed toward it, then, looking left he saw a huge church ahead. *Was this Mission Hill?* He remembered the day he had to go to Peter Bent Brigham Hospital while at Northeastern and he had taken a short walk up this hill. The hospital was only a few blocks away.

Tremont Street was up ahead, then left. The hospital would be a safe haven.

He started to jog. *No, that's not smart, it would call attention to him. Got to slow down, walk naturally.*

He suddenly became aware that he was the only Caucasian on the street. He began walking faster.

Several cars went by. A voice called out. "Hey! Whitey! What the fuck are you doin' out here? You lost?

He looked back. Three black men got out of the car and began walking after him. He started to run. Huntington Avenue was a block away. He could hear them gaining on him, laughing and shouting.

Keep it together. Just a little further. He flew across the intersection just in front of a passing T-train proceeding west. It essentially cut off his pursuers.

Out of breath, he slowed down slightly and made his way up the inclined driveway to the hospital entrance. Safely inside, he turned to see that the three men were heading back to their car. He proceeded to a pay phone in the lobby.

Still clutching the briefcase under his arm he wedged himself into the phone booth and made an anonymous call to the Boston Police Department telling them where Alan's car was.

There was no phone at the camp so he called Judy's residence in Pondvale. He figured they must have somehow gotten back by now.

Alan picked up the phone on the first ring to avoid disturbing everyone else who was sleeping. It had been so late when they got back Judy had persuaded him to stay and sleep on the couch.

"Alan! Thank God! I was stolen!" Bobby proclaimed.

"And so was my car, apparently. Are you o.k., Bobby?"

"Yea, I'm alright. I'm back in Boston?"

"Back? In Boston? What do you mean?"

"It's a long story, Al, and I'll relate the exciting details to you as soon as I can. Suffice to say, mission accomplished, and it was all green, as in cash. You should also be getting your car back in reasonably good shape . . . except for a bullet hole or two."

"Bullet hole? Did you say bullet hole?"

"Hey, no sweat Al. It could have been worse. By the way, how did you get back?"

"By cab. Only 97 bucks. What a deal," Alan joked.

"Hey, that's classy, Alan. By the way, I'm at Peter Bent Brigham Hospital, and no, I'm not a patient, thank God. I'm calling from the lobby, and I think I'm going to find a couch in a waiting room somewhere to curl up on and catch a few winks. In the morning I may just go over to Peter Fuller's and purchase that car I promised I'd pick Carlos up with. By the way, we can't have a self respecting golf pro driving around in a bullet riddled car. You'll have to pick one out for yourself when I get back."

"Hey, Bobby . . . are you shitting me, or what? Be careful, will you?"

CHAPTER FIFTEEN

A week remained and he wasn't sure he could make it. A few days ago, Carlos had picked up a new cell mate . . . a very special cell mate. A specialist in tongue loosening chosen by Bronski. Someone who knew all the little nuances of torture that didn't leave a mark on a person.

Simon Chew was a brute of a man who stood 6'-3" and weighed almost 300 pounds. His hands were like catcher's mitts and when he grabbed Carlos by the balls, it was more than he could bear. Although he knew nothing of what Simon wanted, he had thought that he might be better off just to make something up. Anything to keep the man from beating up on him.

There were many stories going around concerning Simon. Word was that he made it to Concord by releasing a man he was contracted to kill by his ankles . . . ten floors up.

Carlos had pleaded for help from his Latino friends and they had agreed to help him, but nothing had happened. He sensed that his life was in danger, and he needed help fast. He could no longer sleep, and was eating like a bird. He had to hang on. He was so close to walking free from this nightmare of an existence that he didn't dare to jeopardize his release by even talking to any of the friendlier guards. He couldn't trust anyone.

That evening before supper Simon had shoved a towel in Carlos's mouth before he grabbed him by the hair and lifted him slowly off the floor. The pain had been excruciating, and it had happened just before everyone was to file out for the evening meal. Seconds after Simon had left for one of his favorite pastimes he ran his fingers over his bloody scalp, moistened the towel and attempted to clean up.

He had no desire to attend supper that night, but he knew if he didn't, questions might be asked. On the way to the mess hall he became sick, and stumbled several times. Walking through the food line nauseated him.

Upon picking up his food, he found a seat, straddled his tray with his elbows, and put his head in his hands.

Three tables in front of him he could see the parallel folds of skin on the back of Simon Chew's ugly bald head. Simon was busy inhaling the swill they had served that night like it was caviar. Carlos hoped that he might choke on it, but there was little chance of that.

Just when he had decided he'd better eat something, a fight started a few tables behind him. He turned with everyone else to see trays and fists flying, but the guards were quick to quell the disturbance. Two inmates were ushered out, two of Carlos's friends. He was puzzled because he had never recalled the two ever arguing before.

He returned his attention to his food wondering if he would find out what it was all about. He happened to momentarily glance ahead to Simon, who was strangely inanimate and slumped forward. The prominent folds on the back of his neck were smooth. He was now alone at the table which had been previously occupied by several other inmates . . . and he was alone for a reason. His spoon was clenched tightly in his right hand, and his fork . . . his fork had been trust through his windpipe, almost through to the back of his thick neck.

So, the fight had been a diversion, and the kill had been made for him. He experienced a sudden sense of relief, followed by a sickening nervous release that culminated in such shaking that he felt it necessary to quickly grasp the bench he was sitting on for dear life.

The mess hall was cleared immediately as additional guards were brought in.

Following a brief investigation it was never determined who had forked Simon Chew, but while Carlos was being questioned he got sick again and the prison doctor was called in to treat him. He was taken to the prison hospital for evaluation.

While he was in the hospital, the mental anguish began taking a heavy toll. He began to worry about what Bronski's next move would be. He thought it strange, but he almost wished he was back in the relative security of his cell, and yet, it had not proved to be a safe haven. Here in the hospital he felt unprotected, and very vulnerable.

Who might Bronski's next confidant be, the man in the adjoining bed, a nurse, the doctor? The paranoia was building. He tried to focus on his family, his dear sister Placida, and then, Bobby. Would he really be there on his release day, in a Cadillac, no less. He smiled and tried to close his eyes. *You've got to relax*, he told himself.

It was quiet, almost too quiet. There were only two other patients in the ward. Someone who allegedly had his leg broken for him was lying in traction a few beds up from him. A terminal cancer patient was further up the aisle near the nurses station.

His eyes popped open again. He had forgotten to read the letter he had received that day. He had folded it, placed it in his shirt pocket and totally forgotten about it. He reached over to his shirt, pulled it out and snapped on his reading light. The convict with the broken leg stirred slightly as he tore open the envelope.

April 15, 1969

My Dear Carlos:

Your mother, Placida and myself await your release with eager anticipation. It has been an agonizing ten years for us, and I cannot imagine what it has been like for you.

It is said that time heals all wounds, but I am sure that all our hearts have been scarred for life.

Today is also the eighth anniversary of that day when Cuba's brave sons were on their way to the homeland to free it from the tyranny of Fidel Castro.

Last night at our organization meeting we were all very proud to have Pepe San Ramon and Erneido Oliva of the Brigade speak to us. As you know, they were both heroes of the unsuccessful Bay of Pigs invasion, and they continue to prepare themselves for our next attempt to wrest our proud country from the wasteful leadership of Castro.

Not long after they were released from prison they joined the armed forces of the United States in order to keep their minds and bodies in the best possible condition.

Yet, their hearts and souls are also scarred from the experiences of that most unfortunate debacle. The only real cure for their wounds will be to return again someday.

As they recounted their experiences once again, their narration was replete with the many 'if only's and 'why?'s and 'how could it have happened?' that punctuated the entire operation.

They still speak with the highest regard for one of the best friends that free Cuba had, former President John F. Kennedy. May his soul be resting comfortably with God.

They continue to say, that in spite of very poor planning, he should not have been held responsible. In fact, they say that he saved their lives by keeping pressure on Castro while their fates hung in the balance while in prison.

Carlos, there are times when I wish with all my heart, that I was a younger man, but all I can offer now is my financial support for a free Cuba. I hope that when you return, you can also become involved.

The sad truth is, now that Castro is so strongly allied with the Soviet Union, a new invasion is hardly possible.

Stay strong, my son, you are still young, and you will have ample opportunity to make up for lost time.

Love,

Papa

Carlos returned the letter to his shirt pocket, turned off the light and smiled peacefully. His family's letters had been essential to his perseverance during the past ten years.

Through his half opened eyes the room looked somewhat surrealistic and tilted. The security light was casting angular shadows made by the barred windows throughout the room. It was not at all comforting, nor was the intravenous line they had placed in his arm, making it difficult to change positions in bed.

He was not sure why he had qualified for the intravenous fluid, but they assured him it was to be removed in the morning. However, he could stand it no more. He disconnected it and clamped the line, keeping it under the sheet.

He laid there for almost an hour trying to get to sleep and was just about to nod off when he heard footsteps. Someone was rapidly coming down the corridor, past the cancer patient, past the patient in traction. He squinted at the psychedelic appearing figure through half closed eyes, and suddenly became frozen with fear. He could see that the figure had a hypodermic needle in his right hand, and was coming right for him.

He lay as still as he could and feigned a slight snore. For an instant he thought about lunging at the figure, but lying on ones back is not a very effective combative position, and he was still very sore. It was too late now anyway. The figure was bending over him, about to insert the needle into . . . a port on the intravenous line! The person extruded the liquid in the needle quickly, turned, and headed back.

Holy Mary and Jesus, he thought. *What effect might the liquid be having on his system if he hadn't disconnected the line? Think! Think! What might it have been? Poison? Sodium Pentathol?* He would have little time to ponder, the figure was returning, or was it someone else? Yes, the first person had been rather tall. The new figure was short and stocky, and was dressed in a surgical gown and mask. It was indeed a very familiar figure, and Carlos could detect the slight smell of garlic and body odor as the individual bent over him. There was no question . . . it was Bronski.

"What is your name?" Bronski asked.

That's it, thought Carlos, *it must have been some sort of truth serum. Perhaps he could turn the situation to his advantage.*

"My name is C-A-R-L-O-S . . . C-A-R-L-O-S ALMEDA," he slurred

"Ten years ago, you and your friend Bobby Makison were involved in a killing. Is that true?" asked Bronski.

"Yes, it is true."

"When your friend Bobby ran from the nightclub that night he was carrying something, wasn't he?"

"Yes, I see him now, he has a package."

"What became of that package?"

Carlos did not answer.

"What became of that package?" Bronski asked again impatiently.

"My friend Bobby hid it in his apartment."

"Where? Where in his apartment?"

"I do not know. He never told me. He never told me where."

"You're lying, you son-of-a-bitch," said Bronski as he pressed his face closer to Carlos's face. His breath was almost more than he could stand.

"I do not lie," replied Carlos.

"Shit!" he uttered in a muffled tone, "Damn it to hell," he said as he turned and walked back up the aisle.

ыIAKI

CHAPTER SIXTEEN

Bobby spent the night in the relative security of the waiting room at Peter Bent Brigham Hospital with the musty brief-case as a pillow. Several times during the evening he had been aroused by nurses inquiring who he was waiting for. He simply said his wife was being transferred from the local hospital in his home town and since he worked in Boston he decided to wait rather than drive all the way home first.

He awoke in the morning with a terrible sinus headache, obviously caused by his allergies. Somehow it just didn't matter. Not today. Today he had other things on his mind. He tucked the briefcase under his arm and headed for the snack bar in the lobby where he fortified himself with a doughnut and a cup of coffee.

He couldn't wait to call Carlos at the prison to tell him of their good fortune. Glancing at his watch he decided it would probably not be a good time, since the inmates would be having breakfast. He couldn't wait.

Paranoia was setting in. People were beginning to stare at the briefcase, and then at him.

He approached the hospital front entrance very cautiously, scanning for any suspicious looking individuals who might be lurking about. Everyone appeared to be scurrying in and out with an intended purpose.

Two cabs were parked out front. The driver of the lead cab appeared to be dozing off at the wheel like he might have had a rough night driving around the city. Bobby didn't care, he just wanted to get moving. When he opened the back door to get in, it startled the driver.

He had seen an ad by an automobile dealership in one the Boston papers in the waiting room. "Can you get me over to B.U.?" he asked the driver.

"Oh, yes sir, very fine sir. It will be a great pleasure sir," the dark complected driver said as he looked back at Bobby in his rear view mirror and then tipped it down slightly to get a better look at the unusually moldy looking briefcase at his side.

Bobby was taken aback by the drivers politeness. Not at all the usual response uttered by a Boston cabby. He had a sense that this particular driver might also be adept at finding his way around New Delhi or Cairo, but it was his constant peering into the rear view mirror that made him feel most uncomfortable.

It was then that he realized he wasn't dressed much neater than his briefcase. His clothes were dirty and wrinkled from being tossed about in Alan's trunk. His hair was matted down , he needed a shave, and the cut on his nose needed a dressing. He must have presented quite an interesting study for the cab driver who had probably seen just about everything.

"You were at the hospital concerned about some friends who were in the same accident perhaps?" asked the driver, "I hope everyone is going to be alright."

Bobby was relieved. *So that's what this guy had on his mind.*

"You are very perceptive, my friend. That's exactly what happened and, thank you, everyone is going to be fine."

"Well, of course, I do not know what caused the accident, but if the driver was as tired as I am, I certainly would understand. You will be my last fare, my good man, because I must go home to get some sleep."

The drive through Brookline was not long and as the cab came within eyesight of Boston University Bobby began fishing for the smallest bill he could find in the briefcase. *Good God! A hundred dollar bill?*

Arriving in front of the administration building Bobby handed the bill to the driver and saw him grimace with the thought of making change for it.

"I want you to have it . . . all of it, and please be careful driving back to the garage."

The driver was stunned. The meter showed $7.50. Obviously Bobby's appearance had completely mislead him into thinking that he might not even have enough money for the fare.

"God be with you sir! And your family also! The next time you need a cab in Boston, please call me," he said as he gave Bobby his card and drove off exulting in his unexpected good fortune.

Bobby had decided that the first thing he must do was to transfer the money to a less conspicuous looking conveyance. He quickly headed for the university bookstore where he purchased a book back pack. Feeling only slightly guilty about temporarily switching college alliances he also purchased a B.U. sweatshirt to pull over his sad looking shirt.

He then proceeded to the library where he found an unoccupied study cubicle. He quickly counted out $15,000 and transferred the remaining amount of money from the briefcase to the knapsack. Tipping the briefcase upside down to make sure he had removed all of the contents a sealed manila envelope with no outside markings fell out onto the table and he hastily placed it inside the knapsack with the money. He still had no idea of the amount of money, but obviously this was not the time to find out. He would bequeath the moldy briefcase to a rubbish container in the outside corridor.

Joe College proceeded to slick his hair back with his hand and casually stroll out the front door with his knapsack on his back and his pockets slightly bulging with greenbacks. He looked like a happy camper as he strode down Commonwealth Avenue smiling at all the pretty coeds as they passed. *If they only knew*, he chuckled to himself.

He headed for a group of payphones just off the sidewalk and wiggled his hand through the paper money in his pocket to get to some coins. It was time to call Carlos.

After several unsuccessful attempts to reach him, Bobby was finally told that Carlos had been transferred to the prison hospital, and they connected him.

"This is the infirmary. May I help you?" a voice replied.

I've got to be careful, he thought, *maybe I'll arouse less suspicion with a Latin accent.*

"Hello? Who is calling please?" the voice asked again.

"Si! I 'ham Carlos Almeda's father, and I 'ham told he is ill. May I please speak with heem?"

"Wait a moment, please," replied the voice, as several minutes passed.

"Hello! Hello! Father? Is that you?" Carlos asked excitedly.

"Well... not exactly," replied Bobby, and Carlos recognized the voice immediately.

"Look, I know you can't talk," said Bobby, "so just listen. Are you alright?"

"Yes father. Just a minor accident. I will be ready to meet you on my release day on Friday at 10 o'clock."

"O.k., that's great! And I have some exciting news for you. I'll be there on Friday. You can count on it," replied Bobby.

"Si, papa, but you may be in danger now. You must be 'on guard'. You should not buy that car until I help you. I have saved a little money."

"Ok.... o.k., I understand the 'on guard ' bit. Man, do I understand. Take care of yourself, good buddy. I'll be there!"

God damn it! There's more going on that he couldn't tell me. He's in trouble, and it's got something to do with that prick Bronski.

* * *

It's fairly certain that the automobile dealership across the avenue from B.U. has had its share of interesting and famous customers, but the day that the unshaven man with the B.U. sweatshirt and the knapsack came in and plunked down $14,999 in cold, moldy cash for a brand new flame red Cadillac Fleetwood would certainly rank among the more bizarre. And there's one thing that plunking down hard, cold cash will do. It totally circumvents the need to delve into a persons finances and life history.

Bobby knew full well that buying the new car would be the ultimate tip-off to Bronski, but somehow he just didn't give a shit. Following a quick trip to the Registry he was quickly tooling along on Storrow Drive out to Route 2 headed home to Hillston to stash the money.

He wanted to stop at the prison on the way by, but he knew it was too risky. What in hell was Carlos doing in the hospital, and what was this minor accident all about?

It just so happened that as he was driving by the prison , a man in a beat up old Ford Fairlane was coincidentally pulling out of the personnel parking lot. Bobby didn't notice him, but the man driving did a double take when he saw the flashy red Caddy going the other way. That man was Steve Bronski who was headed toward Boston to follow up on the wild goose chase that Carlos had set up for him the night before.

Bobby proceeded around the rotary in front of the prison and continued heading west, thinking about how much he missed Linda, and how lucky he was to have met her. She would also share in their good fortune. Carlos, he had decided long ago would get half, and there would be plenty left over to pay for Alan's wrist operation and the medical bills for Judy's mother. He could also pay for some better treatment for his father. He was almost becoming giddy just thinking about all the good this tainted money could do.

The first thing he must do was to find a secure hiding place for the money. Depositing it in a bank would arouse too much suspicion, and he wasn't at all sure that Bronski was the only one that had a faint clue that it existed. He would head for the camp, count the money, and hide it before he did anything else.

It was a smooth ride out to Hillston and Bobby drove a few miles further west and pulled on to the rutted dirt road leading to the camp. It had been a gray, overcast day with occasional rain that had wet down the dust usually prevalent on the road. There was very little activity around the pond, which would be to his advantage. Alan would be at the golf course. There would be no one around.

He pulled up to the rear of the camp and walked up to the porch with the knapsack in his arms. He thought that he should be more excited about counting the money, but it was almost anti-climactic at this point. He suddenly felt more relaxed than he had a right to feel. The pond was serene and very quiet as a light drizzle continued to fall. His mind drifted back to similar days when he was young and never took the time to stop for a moment to reflect on the beauty of the scene.

There was a particular spot over there on the pond where the pickerel went nuts on days like this. He could hear a big old bullfrog calling out from that same location, calling him to come on over. Probably a descendent of the one he heard years ago.

Bobby stood by the porch almost transfixed, scanning the pond, and listening. He could almost envision old Mr. Marnane slowly swimming back and forth in front of his little cabin across the way. He used to wonder how he could stay afloat he swam so ploddingly, his arms moving in a slow motion Australian crawl. It must have done him some good, he lived to be 80 years old.

A screen door slammed a few cottages down serving to rescue him from his temporary trance, and he proceeded up the steps into the camp.

MAKI

He cleared the long dinner table, and dumped out the contents of the knapsack. He carefully arranged the money in stacks upon the table, and then noticed the manila envelope that had come to his attention while he was hastily transferring the money at B.U. Not thinking any more about it than his initial observation he began counting out the money.

When he was through, the total came to $1,485,000 in American money. Exactly $15,000 short of a million and a half dollars. But there was also some Cuban money, and he had no way of determining how much it was.

He was stunned. *What in God's name had that guy been buying for this kind of money? This wasn't drug money. This was big stuff. This was money on an international scale.*

Suddenly his relative calm was disrupted by new fears. That same paranoia was building again. It caused him to look outside the window at the same time a squirrel jumped onto the camp roof from a nearby tree, and he nearly jumped out of his skin. When his heart rate slowed to near normal again, he quickly began to stuff the money back into the knapsack.

He got everything in, except for the envelope. He paused looking at it, wondering if it was even worth opening, and then his curiosity got the best of him. Using his jackknife he carefully slit the right edge of the envelope open only to reveal another sealed white envelope with the word 'Bcero' hand written across the flap. He recognized the word as being Russian only because he had done some research in prison to determine if there were any similarities with the Finnish language.

He was momentarily stumped. *Bcero . . . Bcero, what in hell does it mean. Of course, it means 'good luck'. But why?*

He carefully tore the same edge of the white envelope open. Inside he found several pages of chemical formulas, a sketch of some sort of missile or canister with very precise dimensions, and a small topographical map of a series of hills and rivers with Spanish names. A word that looked liked 'Sierra' was partially cut off on the right side of the map.

There was no longer any doubt that he and Carlos had become involved in something of far greater magnitude than a drug transaction. Whatever it was, it was obvious that the Soviet Union and Cuba were the main players.

Suddenly, he thought he heard a car engine a distance away.

He quickly placed the documents back in the two envelopes and placed it in the knapsack with the money. Exiting the camp, he moved briskly down to the concrete and stone pillar on the right side of the entrance to the beach. He sat for several minutes on the stone steps looking around for any signs of an observer. Seeing none, he squatted down and removed the loose stone at the base of the pillar that secured the inner void. The knapsack just fit. There was little room to spare. He replaced the stone and spread some beach sand around the base. It would do for now.

The implications of what he had discovered in the envelope were beginning to weigh heavily on his mind. This wasn't just a Bronski thing anymore.

He now realized that he would need to do something with the car. Buying it at this point in time had been much too compulsive. Maybe he could lend it to Alan for awhile. He could keep it parked in the golf course parking lot where it would look less conspicuous, and he might still use it, just to pick up Carlos as he had promised.

CHAPTER SEVENTEEN

Jim Heniger was marking his fifteenth year with the Bureau. Early on in his career he had been assigned to the Boston office, but had since moved on to bigger and better things at Headquarters in Washington.

He had met and married his wife, Stacy, in Boston, and she had given birth to their first child there. He had commuted for almost a year from Boston to Washington until they finally decided to purchase a home in Alexandria where their second and third children were born. Life was good at the Bureau, and traveling was a minimum. He had been assigned to ballistics and was now chief of the lab.

When his Division Chief called him that morning in May he had anticipated a discussion on a routine in-house matter. He was always eager to update his boss on whatever cases were hot at the moment.

His boss, Ed Ditmar, was from the old school, and had actually worked with J. Edgar at some point early in his career. It was no surprise that he was well known for his stories about some of Hoover's escapades.

"Come in, Jim. Please have a seat. Tell me, how are Stacy and the kids?"

Jim was always impressed with Ed's eloquent oak paneled office. It was quite a contrast to a working supervisor's office. His office was in a corner of the lab, and usually strewn with technical books and reports. As the older Division Chiefs retired, so went their ostentatious offices. Jim was convinced that they would probably carry old Ed out and put a 'Museum' sign on the door. He was approaching 40 years with the Bureau and showed no signs of retiring.

"Stacy and the kids are doing just fine, Ed. Thank you for asking."

"They're a great family," Ed replied, gazing reflectively out the window. His career had always come first and had gotten in the way of several relationships. Keeping in touch with the progress of his subordinate's families was a way of filling that void.

"Well, it occurs to me that you've got three potential agents for the Bureau there. It might be time to start nurturing their interests along those lines," Ed said chuckling.

"Right now I think I've got the makings of two firemen and a nurse, but you know how kids interests change, Chief," said Jim as he scanned the enormous office filled with plaques of commendation and pictures taken with high Federal officials. One particular 8x10 showed him shaking hands with President Harry S. Truman.

"Yeah, it's been awhile, but I do remember. Say, Jim, how's that Olson case coming along? Made a match yet?'

It was obvious to Jim that the Olson case would probably not be the subject of today's little meeting. It was much too routine to warrant any extended discussion at Ed's level, but he was impressed that he was familiar enough with his case load.

"Yes, Chief, we got a match from one of the bullets the guys dug out of the wall. I'll have a report to you this afternoon if you'd like."

"Jim, that's great! I'm very happy with the work your people are doing down there, but I'm in no hurry for that report, and it's not why I called you in here today."

"What can I do for you, Chief?" Jim asked cautiously.

Ed walked toward the window with arms crossed, stroking his chin, as if looking at a distant object. His brow was furrowed.

MAKI

"Well, it seems there have been some new developments in a case you had something to do with up in Boston about ten years ago. Our people up there thought that you might be able to fill in some of the cracks. Do you remember the Raoul Hidalgo case?"

"Raoul Hidalgo? Yes, I do. He was the Castro operative who was supposed to make a pickup of a rather large sum of laundered money supplied by the Soviet Union. As I recall this Hidalgo fellow was a former KGB operative who had successfully defected to this country and he was intimidated into performing the money drop because some of his relatives in Moscow were being threatened. As I recall there were a couple of college students who got caught up in it, and the money just disappeared."

"That's right, Jim. A young lad by the name of Bobby Makison and his friend Carlos Almeda ended up doing ten years apiece at Concord Reformatory. It seems Makison has been out for a few weeks, and he's just purchased a brand new $15,000 Cadillac. ..but I wish the case were as simple as the money."

"What do you mean?" Jim asked, becoming increasingly uneasy in the large leather chair.

"Well, we've received information that there might have been something else in with that money."

"Something else?"

"Yes, Jim, apparently there was some technical information regarding the establishment of a top secret germ warfare laboratory the Cubans were in the process of building somewhere in the Sierra Meastra. Apparently the Soviet scientists had been supplying Cuba with the specifications and this was the last piece of the puzzle, so to speak. I guess they figured that their information was going to be as safe as the money, and it was going to the same place."

"It's been ten years, Ed. Can we speculate that the Cuban's have probably received that information by other means by now?"

"Yes, Jim, you may be entirely correct, but the CIA still doesn't know were the facility is. Their flyovers just haven't been able to pick up anything. It's too heavily forested, and they are certain it's underground."

"Those mountains are pretty close to our base in Guantanamo, aren't they?"

"Yes, they are, and that's all the more reason for our concern."

"And you think this information might possibly include a map of some kind?"

"There's a chance, and that's the problem. The Soviets knew that information was with the money, and so did Cuba. This Bobby Makison has unwittingly just run a bright red pair of skivvies to the top of the flagpole for all to see."

"It sure looks like we'd better get to him and that information before someone else does, Chief. As I recall though, there was no evidence to suggest that he had discovered any money at the scene, or anything else for that matter. He didn't come from a wealthy family. Could he have made the money to purchase the car in prison?"

"They tell me he was a real straight arrow in prison, even picked up a law degree. Made a few dollars giving legal advice, but never got involved with black marketing or drugs. He was clean as a whistle, and so was his friend Carlos, who is due to be released this week. The car dealer was quoted as saying that Makison came in with a knapsack, but the money he paid for the car with was separate. A stack of moldy $100 dollar bills."

"That certainly would indicate that the money might have been stashed away for a number of years, but why would he be so obvious?" asked Jim.

"A man who has just spent ten of his best years in prison has a different set of values than you and I, Jim."

"But, this guy isn't your common, ordinary run of the mill criminal. He's supposed to have some smarts. Christ, he'll bring every petty thief who thinks he might have an easy score down on his back."

"That's true, Jim, and that's just another reason why we need you up in Boston for a few weeks to try and locate him."

"Even if he has the money, hasn't the statute of limitations run out on it?" asked Jim.

"Legally, I suppose it has, but the Boston office is aware of several former Castro operatives in the area, and it's no secret that they need money down in Havana. More importantly if there is some secret information about that laboratory, they wouldn't hesitate to kill for it."

"Chief, it's been a long time since I did any field work," said Jim, knowing full well that wasn't going to be the problem. The problem would be being away from Stacy and the kids. The entire family had become spoiled since his assignment as Chief of Ballistics.

"I know that , Jim, but I also know that you were good at it, and hopefully you can get this thing cleared up in a few weeks. We've already made reservations for you at the Statler in Boston. You're to take the shuttle tomorrow morning. Check in with the Boston office when you arrive. Good luck, and be careful." There was a finality in his voice.

Jim summoned up half a smile before leaving Ed Ditmar's office. Most government job descriptions contained the well known phrase, "other duties as assigned", but of all the dumb luck, this assignment took the cake. Sure, it made sense that they would want someone from Headquarters up there, particularly someone familiar with the case, but running a laboratory was a far cry from this cloak and dagger type of operation. His only consolation was that he might be able to wrap it up quickly.

One thing was certain. Stacy was not going to like it, and he would have his work cut out for him even before he got on that plane tomorrow.

CHAPTER EIGHTEEN

"Someday I'm gonna own one of them fucking Cadillacs like that one that just passed by me, or maybe one of them fancy foreign shitboxes like a Saab, no . . . make that a Mercedes.

"Yeah, I think I'm on to something with this fucking caper. No more small time action. This is it! What Carlos burped up on that serum confirms what I read from the newspapers and court transcripts. I knew there was money involved, and now I'm sure of it, but I gotta move fast," Bronski exclaimed to himself through pursed lips as he sped toward Boston.

"No more penny-anti scams. No more shakedowns. Shit, no more job if I can make this score," he mumbled as his car shuddered and skipped pulling away from a stoplight.

"I wondered if that God damn serum was still good. That fucking scene was right out of the movies," he snickered, "Christ it was almost ten years ago I stole that stuff."

He had actually used the serum once before on an old girl friend. A huge smirk came upon his face as he thought about how he had almost killed her administering too large a dose. But it had worked, and he got the information he needed.

"Nobody crosses Steve Bronski. Not my old man, and especially not some hustling broad."

Yet, there was a slight tinge of sadness in his recollection of the hustling broad, Sweet Mary, as he had called her. She was probably the only woman who had ever cared for him, including his mother. The only mistake she had made was trying to change him. When she decided too late that it wouldn't work, she started seeing someone else behind his back . . . an ex-con, no less.

After she had divulged her lovers name, he had gone after him with a vengeance and smashed his jaw so bad he had to eat out of a straw for six months. The incident had intensified his hate for cons.

The Bronski's had originally moved to Massachusetts from the mid-west. His father had been a supply sergeant in the Army stationed at Ft. Devens. He had been a big man and he took his authority home with him at the end of the day. He beat Steve frequently. He strongly recommended that Steve enlist in the Army in order to get straightened out, as he put it. When he refused, the beatings got worse. He was considered a failure by his father.

His brother had made the situation worse. He had graduated from the University of Michigan with a business degree and had become very successful back in the Detroit area. The apple of his father's eye.

A few months before Steve's father was to be discharged he had been diagnosed with angina. One Sunday his father had been watching the Boston Patriots play on television when he experienced chest pain. Steve had been the only one home with him. He called Steve to get a pill from the medicine cabinet. It took 30 minutes for him to get the pill, and he made sure it took that much time for his father to die. Ultimately he placed the pill in his deceased father's mouth for effect. No effect. He lived comfortably with the memory of that last painful, pleading expression on his father's face.

Bronski proceeded down Storrow Drive along the Charles River, swung off at the Massachusetts Avenue exit and headed south through heavy traffic, cursing all the way. He parked his car in a spot on Symphony Road and proceeded to walk over to St. Botolph Street where Bobby and Carlos had shared a room.

The old brownstone should have been down the street one block, but when he got there he discovered that the entire block had apparently been demolished and replaced with one of Northeastern's new dormitories. He was bullshit, but there was nothing he could do. He could see what the original building must have looked like by viewing the adjoining buildings.

Getting in to such a building would have been easy, as easy as buzzing someone in the building from the entry mailbox, and click ... you were in.

The new building, however, required a security card to get in, had security cameras mounted in the foyer, and what would he be able to see even if he got in? It was a dead end, except for one fact, he now had a pretty good idea that Bobby knew where that money was.

Damn it, he wondered, *could he have already picked it up. Was it when I was cold cocked in the Pussy Cat Theater?* He had had some fast talking to do that day trying to convince those two M.P.s that he had tripped and hit his head. He had been out cold for long enough for the little prick to pick up the money.

It had been a long, unproductive trip in to Boston and Bronski was frustrated. He needed a drink. When he rounded the corner on to Mass. Avenue again to walk back to his car the smell of smoke and beer permeated the air in front of Crusher Casey's bar. He would pause only long enough to have a few quick beers to ease his frustration.

When he finally left the bar he was feeling much better about his misfortune. *This may take a little more time than I figured on, but I got plenty of time*, he thought. It was when he was about to cross Huntington Avenue when he felt the presence of someone following him.

Instead of continuing past Symphony Hall, he noticed that the box office was open, so he hurriedly ducked in. His suspicion seemed confirmed when a tall, dark complected man stopped on the street in front of the hall and lit a small, thin cigar. *Who the fuck is this guy?* he wondered. *Who could possibly know what he was doing in Boston?*

MAKI

The man glanced unassumingly up at Bronski, and when he momentarily looked away, Bronski took off like a shot through the large doors to the concert hall. He quickly followed the corridor around the perimeter of the hall to where he found a side door that exited to Symphony Road very near where his car was parked. He started the car and then realized that because the street was one way, he would have to drive very close to the front of the hall where his pursuer had last been seen.

He slowly proceeded up the street with his lights turned off until he was forced to stop at the stop lights before proceeding onto Mass. Avenue, and it was there that the stranger spotted him. Running over to Bronski's car, the man grabbed the door handle on the passenger's side, and had it not been locked, would have been in.

Light, or no light, Bronski decided he had seen enough and he stepped on the gas. He left rubber on the street, and at the same time made a hard left onto Marlboro Street. The stranger's grasp broke free from the door handle and he tumbled onto the street as cars came to a halt in their own symphony of screeching brakes.

Bronski had rarely been so scared in his life. Who was that creep? His competition? A friend of Bobby and Carlos? Maybe this caper was getting a little too dangerous.

No, he had found out too much to quit now. He would need to pursue it further. This might be his most profitable shakedown yet.

It was getting late, but he decided he would head for the Corna Restaurant in Concord. Maybe that sweet little bartender that Bobby had been talking to knew something.

CHAPTER NINETEEN

Bobby was on his way to the golf course to see Alan when a series of sneezes prompted his need to stop at a drugstore to pick up some antihistamine tablets. Just outside the store he spotted a payphone and it occurred to him that he needed to call Linda.

You jerk, he thought, *did you ever think that she might be worried, or might possibly be in danger herself?*

Linda had just left the house for work at the restaurant when she heard the phone ring. She fumbled for her keys to get back into the house as the phone continued to ring. In her haste, she dropped the keys.

Come on! Come on! Be there. Please be there. Bobby mumbled impatiently as the phone continued to ring.

Even if she was taking a shower, she'd have answered by now, he thought, and just as he was about to hang up, she picked up the phone.

"Hello! Hello!" she yelled wanting to ask if it was Bobby, but remembering that she shouldn't.

"Linda! It's me! " he cried.

"Bobby! Bobby! Where have you been? I've been worried sick."

"I'm o.k. I'll have to explain later, but for now you must trust me when I tell you not to go to work tonight."

"What do you mean, don't go to work tonight? They're expecting me. I have to go."

"Linda, things have been happening that lead me to believe that you may be in danger."

"Danger? Why should I be in danger?"

"Very simply, because you know me," replied Bobby. "Look, Linda, do you think you could drive down to the camp tonight. I need to explain what's been going on, and I want you here with me."

"Yes, I can Bobby. It's pretty short notice, but I'll call in sick and leave right away. I should be there in about an hour."

* * *

Just as Linda hung up, an angry Bronski was bumping patrons in the Corna Restaurant like a bull in a china shop as he worked his way down the narrow corridor behind the bar to a seat in the rear. He sat down amidst some indignant stares and ordered a beer.

"Linda working tonight?" he asked the bartender.

"Yeah, she's due in to spell me, as a matter of fact. You a friend of hers?" the bartender asked.

"Well, yes I am . . . I mean, we're taking the same course at Framingham. She said she'd lend me her notes on a class I missed last week," said Bronski.

The bartender's attention was interrupted by the manager who was making her way toward him with a concerned expression behind a smile that begged an answer.

"Oh, shit. I hope this isn't what I think it is," the bartender said in a low voice.

"Dave, would you mind taking the next shift, or even half of it, until I can get someone else in ? Linda's sick."

Bronski couldn't help overhear, and he was pissed, but knew better than to show it.

Dave the bartender hadn't had time to formulate a plausible excuse, and being newly hired, he could only respond affirmatively. "Sure, I guess so," he blurted out, "I'd appreciate it if you could pull someone in for the second half though."

"I'm pretty sure I can get Grace to come in. Thanks Dave, I appreciate it."

"Kinda had you by the balls, did she?" said Bronski looking up from his beer.

The bartender acknowledged his comment with an irritated glance.

"Say, listen, do you happen to know where Linda lives? It's very important that I get those notes from her."

"No. Sorry pal, I couldn't give you that information even if I knew it."

"Look, I could make it worth your while. Would this help?" Bronski slid a partially folded $20 bill toward him.

The bartender glanced at it as he continued washing some beer mugs he had just collected.

"No. I don't think so," he replied.

Bronski reached for a small wad of bills in his pocket and peeled off another $20 and another $10, advancing them toward the bartender.

Dave's eyes widened. He knew that the information the stranger was looking for was in the card file by the cash register. Fifty bucks would sure take a little of the sting out of the extended shift. Why not?

Placing his towel over the money on the bar he picked up both the towel and the money and proceeded to the cash register. Walking over to the register one of the twenties fell on the floor, and in his nervousness stooping over to grab it he cracked his forehead on the tray holding the hard liquor.

Bronski winced. *I hope this young prick doesn't kill himself on his first secret mission.*

The bartender managed to make it to the register without drawing any more attention, looked up and down the bar, and began nervously flipping through the cards in the file.

After a few seconds he starred at one card for what seemed long enough to memorize the book of Genesis. He closed the file quickly at the approach of another bartender.

"Twenty-two Market Street, West Concord," he said to Bronski out of the corner of his mouth.

MAKI

"Where's that?" Bronski asked in a surly manner.

"Shit, man. I think it's just a few blocks south of here. Take a right when you leave the place," the bartender replied hoping the crude individual would leave quickly.

Bronski took his final gulps of beer and was out the door before he had swallowed them. He burped loudly enough out on the sidewalk to be heard back in the restaurant.

Dave was never more happy to see him go, and fully aware that it wasn't college notes the stranger was after. It was then that his conscience began to do a number on him. He hoped that he hadn't put his cohort in any danger. Besides, that cool fifty would but a nice dinner for him and his girl.

It was fortunate for Linda that Bronski decided to walk the few blocks to her aunt's house, because she had left just minutes before he arrived. Linda's aunt was not as fortunate.

Bronski's avarice was feeding his rage as he burst through the rear door to the kitchen at 22 Market Street. Linda's aunt was stirring some soup on the stove, and the instant fear that pulsed at her weakened heart was too much for it. On impulse she was able to grab a carving knife from the nearby rack on the counter in an attempt to fend off the advancing figure, but already the steady frequency of heartbeats that sustained her tenuous existence was gone. She raised the knife as Bronski had stopped his advance, realizing his mistake. She clutched her breast. White faced, she slumped to the floor.

CHAPTER TWENTY

As soon as Linda walked into the camp Bobby realized that his newfound companionship had blossomed into something more. Above everything else, he had fallen in love with her. When he embraced her, he felt whole, and when he was alone he could not explain the emptiness. A longing, deeper than anything he had experienced in prison.

As he held her in his arms he had no idea how close he had come to losing her. His first kiss was soft, inflaming his passion for her. His next kiss was hard, with tongues searching. He knew in an instant that she was the most important thing in his life.

There eyes met. "Bobby, what's going on?" she uttered softly, hesitatingly pulling away.

"Later, please, Linda . . . I'll tell you later," he said as he kissed her again.

She looked at him with yearning eyes as he picked her up and carried her to the bed he had slept in as a child.

The rhythmic squeaking of the old bed played strangely dissonant against the eerie sounds of the birch trees brushing against the camp in the light breeze. They heard little else but each other's heartbeats.

Later they lay side by side, staring at the exposed rafters above them. One of Bobby's old model planes was still hanging in a far corner of the room covered with dust.

Linda rolled onto her side, brushed Bobby's hair from his forehead and smiled.

"I love you, Bobby Makison," she purred.

"I couldn't possibly express in words how much I love you, Linda. I need you to be a part of my life.

"Now, can you tell me what on earth you have been do-ing during the last 24 hours?"

"Yes, I can. I'm sorry I couldn't tell you more before I left. I was afraid your knowledge of what I was about to do might have put you in greater danger."

Bobby began to unravel the bizarre events that had taken place, culminating with the amount of money that the brief-case had contained.

Linda listened intently and seemed to be totally non-plussed. The only thing that really mattered to her was that he had returned safely.

"I'm afraid this fellow Bronski will stop at nothing to get the money, but we should be safe down here. While I was waiting for you I found my old shotgun and some shells in the closet downstairs. It's under this bed right now."

"I guess you could say we just had safe sex," Linda quipped.

"Yes, we've already had the qualifying event for a shot-gun wedding," Bobby retorted with a smile as he drew her to him and kissed her.

They made love again as light began to fade.

* * *

Bobby had parked his new Cadillac near a sandbank slightly up the road from the camp, and Linda had driven her car into one of the bays under the camp. It was now pitch dark. The quarter moon was becoming obscured by clouds, signaling the approach of rain, and the wind was beginning to quicken as Linda and Bobby basked in their new found sensuality.

There was only one entrance to the camp up a set of wooden stairs to a large screened porch that fronted three glass entry doors to the living room. Their tender embrace became suddenly taut, when those same creaky steps began to respond to the weight of someone slowly making their way up to the porch. There was a push to the screen door at the top of the stairs, but the door would not respond because Bobby had engaged the hook latch.

Until that very moment he had never realized what a puny gesture of security the little latch represented. One could easily push a knife through the screen and disengage the hook, which is exactly what the intruder did as footsteps proceeded onto the porch toward the glass paneled entry doors. Had he thrown the deadbolt. Yes, he had, but would it matter.

He motioned to Linda to slip under the bed as he groped for the old pump shotgun. The floorboards creaked slightly as the camp suddenly fell silent, almost as though it was listening . . . listening for the intruder.

It took no more than a few seconds before a glass panel in the door succumbed to a harder object. Glass played against the floor like the upper registers of a xylophone.

The night air was getting cooler as Bobby poised by the entrance to the bedroom door in the buff. A slight shiver stimulated his naked frame. He could hear the intruder release the deadbolt downstairs. He was in.

Once again, silence, as the intruder might be attempting to adjust his eyes to the darkness? *It might provide some small advantage*, Bobby thought. At least he knew every square inch of the camp in the dark, and there was no mistaking, it was dark. The moon was now totally obscured by clouds and the first evidence of rain could be heard on the camp roof.

Bobby had only one concern now, and that was for Linda's safety. Prison had given him a new sense of his own tenuous existence. It had taught him that life was a day by day proposition. Since meeting her, he was just beginning to look beyond a day. It wasn't about the money or anything else now.

He could hear the intruder cursing the darkness as he stumbled through the downstairs area, occasionally knocking

MAKI

over objects. Now he knew who it was . . . Bronski. For years he had lived with that same filthy cursing.

Bobby knew that there was no turning back for the twisted soul that lurked below him. His obsession for the money had elevated him to a new plateau of evil and he would stop at nothing to get it.

He walked carefully over to the bed, bent over, and held Linda's hand. He gripped it hard, and as he kissed her palm he felt her pulse jumping furiously. He knew he could never forgive himself if anything happened to her, and he cursed himself for putting her in this situation. It would only be a few minutes before Bronski would begin climbing the staircase to the bedrooms.

Would he still retain the element of surprise, he wondered, as he heard the unmistakable sound of footsteps coming up the bare wooden steps. Bronski apparently wasn't quite sure if anyone was in the camp, but there was nothing subtle about his movement, and why no flashlight? It was either the movement of a man who could care less about his actions, or his desire not to call attention to anyone who might be outside the camp.

Just as Bronski reached the top of the stairs a few feet from the doorway to the bedroom, Bobby suddenly remembered he hadn't chambered a shell in the shotgun. He would need time to insert one . . . precious time. He turned toward the nightstand where he had put the shells, a floor board moaned loudly, and like a cat Bronski dove at him. His shoulder caught Bobby in the solar plexus.

Blackness, the descending darkness of a deep abyss quickly enveloped him.

When he awoke, he was on the floor, handcuffed by one hand to the bed frame at the foot of the bed. With his free hand he reached up to his forehead to feel the imprint of the barrel of his shotgun.

Bronski had been terrorizing Linda who was lying spread eagle on the bed. A small lamp glowed low and unobtrusively in the far corner of the room casting a grotesque shadow of Bronski on the wall.

She was crying hysterically, a loose sheet covering her.

"Bobby! Bobby! Thank God you're all right. I tried to get away, but he was too strong. I'm sorry, so sorry."

Bobby felt an overwhelming sense of failure as he strained to lift himself up, only to be knocked down by Bronski.

"Linda, he didn't . . ."

"No I didn't, but I could have, you pathetic little bastard. You know, you gave me a scare for a few minutes. Had to give you a little mouth to mouth to get you breathing again. I sure don't want anything to happen to the man whose going to tell me where the money is. No sir, I was even thinking about extending the courtesy of a little resuscitation on your very pretty young lady, but I wanted you to be fully awake first. I must say you have excellent taste in women, for a punk."

Bronski grabbed a corner of the sheet and whipped it off of Linda. She grimaced attempting to contort her body to hide her private parts.

"You so much as lay a hand on her, and so help me I'll kill you," Bobby screamed.

"Oh, you'll do that, will you. That will be a good trick, won't it, you little prick," replied Bronski as he slugged Bobby in the face breaking his nose.

Bobby was momentarily stunned as he attempted to stem the flow of blood cascading from his nose with his free hand.

"Consider that a little payback for clubbing me in the Pussycat the other day, and don't get any blood in your big blue eyes, because I don't want you to miss what I'm gonna do to your cute little honey."

Bronski took a rotten looking handkerchief from his pants pocket, stuffed it in Linda's mouth, and proceeded to un-buckle his pants.

Linda gagged as Bobby frantically looked around the room for something, anything to grab and throw at Bronski. There

MAKI

was nothing he could reach and could only extend his arm to the lower portion of the mattress.

Linda's eyes grew wide with terror as she watched the ugly, hulking form of Bronski begin to lower upon her.

"You lousy bastard!" Bobby screamed at the top of his lungs just a human form came diving through the bedroom door opening with something raised over its head.

Linda couldn't see what had caused Bronski to suddenly become inanimate, but Bobby could.

"Holy shit, Alan! How long have you been out there," he asked, struggling to catch his breath. He had unconsciously been holding it waiting for the inevitable to happen.

"Hey, you're not forgetting I live here too. When I pulled up and saw a strange car up the road, and that new Cadillac up at the sandbank, I kinda figured something was going on. I parked my car and grabbed a sand wedge out of my golf bag. About the time I got to the camp and saw the broken glass on the porch, I heard voices and proceeded up the stairs. That may have been the best wedge shot I ever made, even though I shanked it a little," Alan said laughing.

Alan quickly rolled Bronski off of Linda, removed the gag from her mouth and covered her with the sheet. She was still too shocked to speak and began to sob.

Bronski had a large contusion on the back of his head, and was starting to moan.

"Quick, Alan. See if you can find the keys to the cuffs in Bronski's pocket. We'll need to get them off of us and on to him before he comes out of it."

Linda was almost catatonic as she turned her head on to a pillow to try and wipe the tears and perspiration from her face. She found herself starring at Bronski's face as drool trickled from the side of his mouth.

Alan had found a key ring attached to Bronski's belt where he had dropped his pants, and was hurriedly trying keys in the handcuffs that bound her. As soon as her right hand was free she became hysterical and hit Bronski in the face again, and again, and again. Bronski stopped moaning.

"Honey, it's over! It's all over!" yelled Bobby as she began to cry uncontrollably.

"There! Now you, little brother," Alan said as he released her from the remaining handcuff. She quickly gathered her clothes and retreated to another room.

They spread eagled Bronski face down on the bed, and used the same cuffs to secure him to the bedposts. A pool of blood was slowly saturating the bedsheet from the wound on his head.

Bobby looked like he had tried to eat a quart of raspberries with his hands behind his back as he embraced Linda. He could feel her body tremble as he gently rubbed her back and neck.

"We'd better get to a phone and report this as quickly as we can. I think the ugly bastard could use an ambulance. At least this should keep him off the street for awhile," said Alan as they bounded down the stairs.

Bobby turned the switch on the old antique floor lamp by a chair that looked like it could use some surgery to keep the stuffing from coming out.

"What was that?" asked Alan as he turned his head toward the stairwell they had just come down.

"What was what?" asked Linda as they all froze, straining to hear.

"Forget it, Alan. Let's just get the hell out of here," said Bobby grabbing Alan's arm, but he was already in motion, and he slipped from Bobby's grasp.

"Take Linda back to the car, Bobby. I'll be right with you," he said as he proceeded back up the stairs.

Except for the light from the downstairs lamp filtering up the stairwell it was still dark in the bedroom where Bronski had been secured to the bed. The small oil lamp in the corner of the room was slowly flickering out.

MAKI

Alan glanced over at the bed. Bronski was stone still, too still. Beside him lay two pillows with protruding feathers and a single hole through them. There was little doubt that some-one had shot him in the back of the head.

Alan turned to run, but got nowhere before a rigid hand chopped down on the back of his neck.

Linda and Bobby had made it back to Bobby's car parked beneath the high, sheer sand cliff at the sandbank.

"Jesus! Where is he!" Bobby asked as he tightly grasped Linda's hand.

After a few minutes it was clear that something had hap-pened to detain Alan.

"I've got to go back, Linda," said Bobby reaching for the door handle.

"No, please Bobby! If that vile man got free he would surely kill you!" she replied trying to restrain him.

"It may be something simple like . . . like maybe he fell down the stairs," replied Bobby. "Look, here are the keys. I want you to drive back to the police station in town. Tell them what happened. Alan and I will wait for you and the police."

"I'm not going to leave you two here alone with that animal!" Linda cried holding on to his arm.

"Linda, please. Alan just saved our lives. Please do as I say. I love you very much and I want you out of here. I'll be alright."

Bobby kissed her, tucked the old shotgun under his arm and started to walk back to the camp. It was beginning to rain heavily and he felt cold, wet and exhausted. His broken nose was throbbing painfully, but he knew he couldn't leave his brother. He kept looking back to the car as he walked along the dirt road, but Linda was apparently not doing as he had asked. He saw no car lights go on.

The darkness combined with the rain pelting on the win-dow obscured her view from the outside world. It was a frightening place and she was still shaking with cold and fear. Maybe Bobby was right. Maybe she should get some help. Besides, she needed the warmth of the car heater.

She started the car, but in her confused state of mind, she put the automatic shift in DRIVE and being only a few feet from the sand cliff, came hard up against it and stopped. Realizing her mistake, she immediately put the shift lever in REVERSE, but it was already too late. The impact had loosened the sand on the forty foot high banking. She could hear the sand slowly slipping down, enveloping the front of the automobile. She gunned the engine. The rear wheels spun furiously, digging deeper and deeper into the sand. She was trapped.

Oh, my God. How could I have been so stupid, she thought, as she was suddenly gripped with panic.

"Got to get out! Got to get out!" she screamed, realizing she was being buried alive.

She pulled on the door handle and pushed hard against the door with her shoulder, harder . . . and harder. It wouldn't budge. She could see the sand against the side window now. It was slowly sifting over the car. Rocks were bouncing off the roof. She was slowly becoming entombed.

Shut of the engine, quick, she thought, *I'll have enough air for awhile, but the carbon monoxide will surely kill me.*

A desperately futile scream, "Help! Help! Bobby please come back! Please help me! " but her screams were totally muted by the tons of sand and gravel enveloping the car.

* * *

A tall, dark complected figure hovered over Alan's motionless body. Drawing his 9mm Glock from his shoulder holster, he quickly attached a silencer and placed the business end at Alan's temple.

"Alan! Alan! Where are you? Let's go, buddy!" Bobby yelled as he trudged loudly up the porch steps.

MAKI

His finger relaxed on the trigger upon hearing Bobby's voice, and he withdrew the gun from Alan's temple. If either of the brothers knew where the briefcase would be, it would probably be this Bobby.

Something obviously went wrong, very wrong. Why isn't he responding ? Better not go upstairs by the stairway. Be a sitting duck. But how? What about the old rope ladder they had made when they were kids. It should be hanging off a birch tree near the second floor porch. Not hardly. Christ , I'm not a kid any more, and that creaky old birch would surely give way. Got to think. If Bronski had recovered enough to somehow overpower Alan, what would get him down-stairs? . . . Of course! The money!

"Hey, Alan, I'm going to grab the knapsack. I'll meet you back at the car," he shouted.

He retreated behind the large stone pillar where he had hid the money. It was only a few steps from the porch steps.

Would it work? he thought, *Please God, make it work.*

He waited in the cold rain wondering if the old shotgun would fire, having gotten so wet. A shiver shook his wet body as he peered up at the porch. The entire escapade had gone much too far. The thought of the money and the good it could do didn't matter anymore.

He stared into the darkness of the porch for so long he almost became mesmerized, and then he saw it, a tall, slim figure moving ever so stealthily onto the porch.

He could tell immediately that it wasn't Bronski's short, stocky form, and when he realized it wasn't Alan, he felt a sickness in his stomach. *Who is this person, and what has he done to Alan?*

The figure moved slowly down the porch steps. Bobby's finger tightened on the shotgun trigger, but the uncertainty of knowing who this man was, caused him to hesitate.

"Hold it right there, pal," he blurted out

The figure froze momentarily, but somehow sensing the uncertainty of the challenger, he whirled.

Bobby felt the impact of something sharp penetrate his shoulder just below his collarbone. The shock pulled the trigger for him.

The pain was intense. A small dagger protruded, several inches of which was now embedded in him. He staggered backward and spotted the man grasping his forehead. He was screaming in Spanish. He had shot high, but apparently some of the buckshot had found its mark.

Bobby fell back onto the beach fighting an overwhelming desire to black out. He tried to pull the knife out, but it was lodged too deeply in his shoulder. He sensed the injury was not life threatening, but a follow-up by the stranger might well be.

He raised his head after what must have been a brief blackout. It was difficult to discern just who, or what it was that was hovering over him with a portion of his scalp missing, and isolated buckshot holes emitting blood throughout the facial area.

"I will give you just a minute to tell me where the briefcase is before I kill you and look for it myself, my friend."

His gun was pointed directly at Bobby's head, and his hand was trembling severely as though he was experiencing the trauma of his very severe injuries. Blood from his horrible head wound mixed with the steady rain was streaming into his eyes as he attempted to improve his vision by running a forearm across his forehead.

Bobby wondered for an instant who this desperate man might be. After a decade of incarceration and several weeks of fear and pain, this man with the gun might be the only one who knew the true story behind the briefcase.

How ironic, he thought, *I may never find out now.*

"Do not strain my fucking patience you little bastard," he bellowed with intent, mixed with obvious pain. "You now

MAKI

have exactly one minute before I put you out of your observable misery and go back to your brother."

"He doesn't know where it is. I never told him. Please don't hurt him," Bobby said between gasps.

"You lying Gringo son-of-a-bitch! Say your prayers!" screamed the man, as his finger tightened on the trigger.

Having no strength to resist or respond, he felt himself slipping back into the same tunnel of unconsciousness... just before he heard the shot.

CHAPTER
TWENTY ONE

On a scale of from one to ten, Jim Heniger's enthusiasm for his new assignment measured as a fraction. His only consolation would be spending some time with his wife's parents on the South Shore. It would be a pleasure for him, and the suggestion had definitely helped to smooth things over with Stacy. She had not been happy when he told her of the assignment. They both realized that they had become spoiled.

He and Stacy were not only still very much in love, but they were each other's best friend, and the kids had gotten used to having their dad come home every night. His being away would be more tiring for her.

As the plane flew over central Massachusetts to make its approach to Logan Airport he closed his eyes and thought about how they had made love last night. She had been unusually passionate, almost as though the ardor carried extra meaning. What he didn't know, was that for the first time in years, she was genuinely afraid for him.

The plane dropped lower out of the heavy clouds that were approaching Boston from the west. It would be a sunny day in Boston for at least a few more hours. Peering from the window he could actually see the quaint little coastal village of Cohasset just south of Boston where he and Stacy had met and fallen in love.

It was just a few more minutes before he heard the familiar, "In behalf of the Captain and the crew we would like to welcome you to Boston. Please keep your seat belts fastened and remain in your seats until the plane comes to a complete stop at the terminal."

He rented a car at the airport and after a few wrong turns coming out of the tunnel from East Boston and a few dozen curse words, eventually he headed south on the Central Artery.

Following a brief visit to Stacy's parents and a call home to let her know he had arrived safely, Jim put on his game face and headed back into Boston to FBI Headquarters.

It was heartwarming to renew some old acquaintances with friends he thought might have been retired or transferred. He was most surprised to find out that almost all of the staff knew who he was, having coordinated with his lab on various cases over the years. Stories had also circulated regarding his exploits while assigned to the Boston office during the Boston Strangler era.

After the usual backslapping and story telling subsided, Jim was assessed of the current situation concerning Bobby Makison and his friend Carlos by Paul Dexter, Chief of the Boston office. Dexter had been a cohort of Jim's and he wasn't at all surprised to see that the 'yes man' had ascended to the top spot.

"Jim, his name is Victor. Victor Delazar from the so-called Cuban CIA. He's one of Castro's most entrusted operators. Trained in the Soviet Union by the KGB, he's considered to be the James Bond of Cuban intelligence.

He had been somewhat of a rebel since birth, and had fallen in love and married a niece of the deposed dictator, Batista. But, in spite of being one of the favored few, he found himself becoming more sympathetic to the cause of his old school chum Fidel Castro.

He had secretly always shared the same discontent and desire for a free Cuba. Needless to say, his inside track to the Batista family had been very valuable to the rebel cause.

He actually graduated from Wentworth Institute six years prior to the incident at the Latino Club, and he knew Carlos from social get-togethers of friends of the Batista family.

He is a master at blending into the American culture. He can be very Bostonian or easily pass himself off as French Canadian, Polish or even Russian because of his fluency with the languages and his expertise with disguises.

He's in the area, Jim, and we have reason to believe he's homing in on Bobby and Carlos."

"How does our CIA fit in to the picture, Paul ?" Jim asked.

"We've been given the green light to go it alone, Jim. I'm assigning you another agent from our office." He asked his secretary to send in Agent Berg.

Jim was initially caught off guard as Agent Berg entered the room.

"Kerstin, I'd like you to meet Jim Heniger from Washington."

He extended his hand to the slightly butch, but disarmingly beautiful young female who approached him. Her hand was small, but her handshake was firm, to say the least. She was a very petite, blue eyed blonde.

"I have heard a lot about you Mr. Heniger and read several of your ballistic manuals."

"Miss Berg was born and raised in Norway until she came over to study at Tufts University. She's also a Harvard Law School graduate, smart as a whip, and one of our best agents," said Paul Dexter as he studied Jim's quizzical gaze.

He would later find out that her young appearance had made her very adaptable to specialized assignments, and on a recent assignment had actually posed as an exchange student. She was an intensely curious young lady who was more comfortable with older men.

To say that Jim was uncomfortable with her, however, would have been an understatement. Now, he would not only have to account for his own actions, he would also be responsible for her.

Upon reviewing the case file it was apparent the only inroad currently available was a visit to Carlos at Concord

MAKI

Reformatory. He was due to be released in just a few days, and then he might be difficult to locate. Kerstin agreed.

"Well Miss Berg. Let's see what we can find out. Are you ready for this?" he asked with a stern, confident smile that belied his own self doubt.

The ride from Boston to Concord is less than thirty minutes. It can be made longer and more scenic if one strays from Route 2 and heads down the same route that Paul Revere and his lesser known compatriots William Dawes and Dr. Samuel Prescott once rode on their way to warn of the British advance.

Jim chose the quicker option, and was almost sure that he had been spared at least a few inquiring questions regarding the science of ballistics along the way.

When they arrived at the prison they met briefly with the warden and then with a very nervous Carlos. He confided that he was concerned for Bobby's safety and was becoming increasingly apprehensive as the time for his release approached. He was sure that something was going to happen to screw up the event .

"Carlos, how would you like to help us find Bobby?" asked Jim.

It had been so long since Carlos had smiled so broadly it almost hurt the corners of his mouth. "Are you kidding. If you can wait a few days, I will be ready!"

"No, Carlos, now . . . we need your help now. Listen, we have already spoken to the warden and received his blessing to release you today."

Carlos was stunned. He stared at Jim and Kerstin for several seconds as tears began to well up in his eyes. Almost simultaneously he became curiously stimulated by the very subtle scent of the perfume Kerstin was wearing. A very interesting combination of emotions. Slightly more thought provoking than the perfume worn by his sister.

"Holy Mother . . . are you kidding! There is nothing on this earth that I wouldn't do to help my good friend Bobby!"

"Well, you can start by telling us where he might be," Kerstin asked with a smile.

"I think he might possibly be at the camp that he often spoke about. It was on a lake just outside his hometown . . . Hillston, I think he called it," replied an exuberant Carlos.

"Yeah, that checks with the file, doesn't it Kerstin?" said Jim, "It's less than an hour from here as I recall. How quickly can you get your things together, Carlos?"

"I don't have too many compadres in this place to say buenos dias to, and my possessions will fit in a shopping bag. They owe me a few dollars for working in the prison shop that I would like to pick up."

"Don't worry, the warden said you had some money coming and he obtained it for us to give to you."

As he spoke, Kerstin's mind had wandered only slightly as she observed the gentle demeanor of the prematurely graying Cuban who's eyes had actually been made more attractive by the lines reflecting his years in prison. He was not what she would have considered stereotypical of an inmate. Based on what she knew of his file, it would be doubtful if he ever saw the inside of a prison again.

"O.k., let's get going, it's getting dark and we'll need all the daylight we can get to locate this place. Oh, by the way, we also picked up your old clothes. Why don't you take a few minutes to get rid of that Brooks Brothers suit you have on."

*　*　*

As they rode through the prison farm, Carlos glanced back through the rear window of the car at the prison where he had spent one-third of his life. Tiny droplets of rain began to obscure his vision and hopefully his miserable existence. There had been times when he had felt very expendable and was sure he might die, but the realization that he was finally

MAKI

free began to slowly sink in. He cupped his head in his hands, and began to weep.

"You all right back there?" asked Jim looking in the rear view mirror.

"I am sorry, my friends. I do not know what came over me. I guess it's the memories. I can't explain it . . . I just . . . I just cannot believe that I am out of that place. Please excuse me," cried Carlos as he wiped his eyes with his sleeve.

Having done some undergraduate work in psychology, Kerstin recognized the symptoms. "You may find yourself doing that on occasion and sometimes very spontaneously. Don't fight it, it's very natural after what you have been through. It's a post-traumatic reaction. Tell me what do you plan to do with your new life, Carlos?"

"Aahh, yes, my new life. Myself and many other Cubans would like to go home, but we cannot. My family was forced to leave their home there, and they now reside just outside of Miami. I am eager to see them again . . . but first we must find my dear friend Bobby. I am afraid he is in grave danger," Carlos replied with concern, "You see, one of the prison guards, a Mr. Bronski is determined that there was some money involved with our crime ten years ago."

"Yes, we're almost sure that there was a briefcase in that Men's Room, Carlos," said Jim looking in the mirror. "We're not exactly sure of the contents of that briefcase."

The rain began to intensify, and as they drove higher into the central Massachusetts highlands it became darker.

"I'll be damned!" Jim exclaimed, "I think my ears just popped. We must be climbing."

Kerstin looked over her shoulder and smiled. Carlos was slumped over in a deep, peaceful sleep.

"We just hit the Hillston town line, Jim. We want Exit 22," Kerstin said as she squinted ahead attempting to make out the next sign. "Let's stop at that gas station ahead and see if we can get some direction from here."

They drove of off the main highway, received some sketchy directions and continued to proceed in a westerly direction toward Kendall Pond. As they turned on to the dirt road to the camp they found it to be a good test of the car's shocks and springs as they jostled along through some sizeable ruts and gullies.

Carlos was rudely awakened when his bobbing head hit the rear door window.

"What the . . . ? Where are we?" he asked as he attempted to look out into the darkness.

"Oh my god! Jim! Look at that car parked in that sandbank! It's rear lights are on, but it's nearly covered with sand," Kerstin exclaimed as their car rounded a severe bend in the road.

"Christ, I hope there's nobody in it, but why would the lights be on?" Jim replied.

He stopped the car and left his headlights shining on it as they all ran toward the partially buried car. Realizing they would need something to dig with, Jim ran back to his car to look in the trunk. All he was able to find was a lantern, a set of hubcaps and a jack handle, which he grabbed and ran back with.

By then, Carlos, digging with his hands, had exposed the back window. The steady rain was mixing with the sand making it extremely difficult to see into the car.

"Mr. Heniger! Bring the light over here!" he yelled.

Jim climbed onto the trunk and shined the light in to see a hysterical young woman looking back from the front seat. She was crying and her lips were moving, but no sound was emanating from her expensive tomb. The tons of sand on the car had provided the ultimate in sound insulation.

Kerstin had been frantically attempting to dig with her hands to uncover a door, but it was hopeless.

"Jim! We've got to get her out of there before anymore sand slips down. It looks like that back window is the only way out!" she said shaking the sand off her hands.

Carlos grabbed the jack handle from Jim and began to swing it at the rear window, but the defrosting wire embedded in the glass acted as reinforcement, and it refused to break.

Seeing Carlos's frustration, Jim picked up a sizeable stone almost a foot in diameter and raised it over his head.

"Look out!" he shouted as he plunged it into the window.

The window shattered as the huge stone bounced off the rear seat onto the floor as the woman in the front seat screamed.

"You must climb over the front seat as quickly as you can," Jim yelled in to the woman.

Carlos began raking the perimeter of the window casing with the jack handle to loosen the remaining shards of glass.

"Hurry! Hurry now!" Jim shouted in again.

The woman was obviously petrified, too afraid to move.

More sand began drifting down from the banking, apparently loosened by the slight movement of the car. Carlos dove over the top of the window placing his body as a barrier to block the deluge of falling sand and stones.

"I do not know how much longer I can hold this sand back, my friends," Carlos shouted as he became half buried himself.

"I've got to go in there and get her," said Kerstin, "She needs to hear another woman's voice," and she hopped up onto the trunk.

"God dammit. Wait!" Jim shouted too late. She was already in.

After a few seconds, a head began to approach the rear window. It was the young woman, followed closely by Kerstin.

When they were both safely out, Jim helped Carlos down from the top of the car. Relief shown on the faces of the trio and there were enough pats on the back to go around. They looked like they had just competed in a mud wrestling contest.

The only one that didn't look too dirty was the young woman, but she wasn't smiling. She was attempting to regain some semblance of sanity.

"Just who are you, young lady, and what in God's name happened?" asked Jim.

Stooped over, with her hands on her knees, she appeared to be hyperventilating slightly as she raised her head to look at her rescuers.

"Thank you. Oh, thank you. You saved my life. I know it . . . you saved my life. I had given up hope, and , well . . . my name is Linda, and my boyfriend is in trouble . . . and well, I was trying to go for help and I must have driven into the sandbank and caused an avalanche. We must get help from the police."

"Wait a minute," Carlos interrupted, "what is you boyfriends name?"

"Bobby . . . Bobby Makison," she replied.

"Buenos noches! I am Bobby's friend, Carlos, and these people are from the FBI. We came to try and find him."

"Oh, Carlos, yes! Bobby has told me so much about you. Do you mind if I hug you. I can't seem to stop trembling."

She put her arms around him and hugged him tightly for several minutes as Jim looked down the dark road contemplating their next move.

"Bobby is in the camp with his brother Alan. He went back to the camp when Alan didn't return. You see, a prison guard by the name of Bronski assaulted us and tied us up, and . . . well, Alan surprised us all and knocked him out. Bobby and I came back to the car, but Alan didn't return, and . . ."

"Wait a minute Linda, slow down now. You mean Alan never came out of the camp, and now Bobby hasn't returned either?" asked Kerstin as she took Linda's hand and started to rub it.

"Yes! Yes! I don't know what happened to them," Linda cried.

Jim looked at Kerstin, and then at Carlos.

"I can't thank you enough for what you did here tonight, Carlos, but I can't let you get involved any further. It could be dangerous, and I need you to stay back with Linda."

Carlos wasn't too happy with the decision knowing that his friend was probably in trouble, but he knew that Jim was right.

"I will be happy to, Mr. Heniger," he replied as he looked over at the half buried car again. "By the way, Linda, that wasn't by any chance the Cadillac that Bobby was going to pick me up in?"

Linda smiled, "Yes, it was Carlos . . . it was."

Jim and Kerstin pulled the weapons from their shoulder holsters, blew some sand from them and gave them a quick check. Jim went back to the car and removed a case containing a rifle and a night scope. He assembled it, and looked at Kerstin.

"Let's go, Miss Berg," and they headed down the dirt road to the camp.

He couldn't help thinking that his fellow agent had been a pretty spunky lady back there, and he now felt very comfortable having her along side.

As they approached the rear of the camp it was completely dark, but they could hear voices that sounded like they were coming from the front, near the pond. They walked quickly along the side of the camp.

Jim saw the two figures first, one standing up with what appeared to be a gun, and the other on his back on the beach. He thought he heard the figure with the gun say something like 'gringo bastard'.

He raised his rifle quickly in order to see more clearly through the night scope. It looked like the tall figure was about to shoot the man on the ground, and when he heard the words 'say your prayers' he knew he must fire.

The shot found its mark as the tall figure fell forward onto the man on the ground.

"Kerstin, check out the inside of the camp, and I'll see who these two are out front," Jim said as he drew his revolver.

With her gun drawn, she moved up the porch steps, paused slightly when the squeaky porch door signaled her entrance, and then proceeded in.

Jim flipped the body of the man he had shot off of the man lying on the ground, and was startled to see the condition of his face. The figure lying on the ground wasn't looking too much better either, except that a check of his carotid artery indicated he was alive.

The heavy rain was playing on the man's face slowly making him more recognizable as it washed away the blood. Jim knelt down to get a closer look, and he could see that he resembled the file photo of Bobby Makison.

"Hey! Hey! Wake up!" he shouted as he jostled Bobby.

Bobby awoke in a panic. His eyes opened wide as he stared up at Jim. "No! No! Please don't," he screamed.

"It's all right, Bobby. It's all over. You're o.k. now. You're safe," Jim repeated in a calming tone.

Realizing that the man kneeling next to him was not the tall stranger who was about to kill him, he relaxed slightly.

"Who are you? Oh my God ! Where's Alan? We've got to see if he's alright. Do you know if he's alright?"

Jim looked up to see Kerstin walk out onto the small second floor porch. "We're secure up here Jim! Got a fellow who says his name is Alan with a nasty head wound, but I think he'll be o.k. The other one up here isn't talking . . . he's pretty dead. Could be that Bronski character Carlos mentioned.

Bobby looked up at the porch and grimaced when he put pressure on the dagger that was still protruding from his shoulder.

"Alan! Alan! Are you o.k.?" he yelled.

Alan walked out onto the porch pressing a bloody towel to the back of his head.

"Yeah, I'm not doing too bad . . . but I'd rather be playing golf," he laughed.

Bobby smiled as his world started spinning again and he slipped back into unconsciousness.

"I'd say it's about time we got some assistance down here, Kerstin. Would you mind going back to the car and calling the locals in with a couple of ambulances," said Jim as he tried to determine what he could do for Bobby.

Kerstin bounded down the porch steps talking to herself. *Man, they're going to love this mess. Probably the most exciting thing to happen in this town since the last Indian war.*

CHAPTER TWENTY TWO

It was one of those typically warm, tropical nights in Miami exactly one year later as two couples and a handsome young man strode down West Flagler Street in a section of the city known as Little Havana,

They were headed for a reunion party at a restaurant called La Tasca operated by a friend of Carlos. Their individual moods reflected their happiness, but they would never forget the experiences that brought them together, and the evening would undoubtedly rekindle many memories.

Alan had received a mild concussion that frightful night at the camp. He had recovered quickly, and a few months later would have the operation on his wrist to repair the nerves that were making it impossible for him to compete. Feeling physically good again and rediscovering Judy and his son, not to mention looking death in the eye, had made a new man of him.

Judy had always understood Alan's compulsive desire to compete, and she had never stopped loving him, in spite of nearly giving up hope that they might never be reunited. She had always wondered if Christopher would ever know his father.

Following his operation and several months of rehabilitation, Alan, Judy, and Christopher headed for south Florida. He became Assistant Professional at Doral Resort and Country Club in Miami. The head pro was an old friend from his previous tour experiences, and had agreed that Alan could round himself back into playing form again while conducting his duties at the club.

In fact, he had successfully completed the tour qualifying school, had obtained his tour playing card, and made a fair amount of money in several events during the spring tour.

Judy had transferred her credits from Boston University to the University of Miami. She was just completing her first year there, and with only a year to go for her B.A. in Music, she already had her sights set on a Masters Degree.

Young Christopher initially had a tough time leaving his friends in Pondville, but was now a true Floridian. He had taken to the warm, sunny climate and the proximity of the Disney attractions almost immediately. He established a whole new group of friends and not lost touch with his northern friends who occasionally stopped by to visit.

Judy and Christopher had already traveled with Alan to a few tournaments, and Christopher was awful proud that his dad could converse with the likes of Arnold Palmer and Gary Player.

The only downer in this wonderful new relationship with Judy and his son had been his current wife, Beth. She had been so adamant about dumping Alan, until she had gotten wind of his good fortune, and was now stalling the divorce proceedings. Somehow, however, it just didn't seem to matter to Judy and Alan. They knew that someday, they would be husband and wife.

Mr. and Mrs. Robert Makison were just a few steps behind, strolling arm in arm, and looking very much in love. It was still very painful for Bobby to recall where he had been for the past decade. It was more difficult to recall the incredible culmination of it all.

His shoulder would never be quite the same, because the dagger had penetrated so deeply into tendons and muscle. Interestingly enough, his doctor had recommended he take up golf for additional therapy.

He quickly discovered that becoming a practicing attorney as a convicted felon was not going to be easy. He had gathered some good commendations from the prison and Professor Bingham. Jim Heniger had also put in a good word for both he and Carlos, but his case was still pending before the State Board of Attorneys. In the meantime he had procured a position as a Title Examiner with the state and he was a very happy man.

Linda had a difficult time overcoming the mental trauma of nearly being raped and buried alive. She spent several months in therapy with a psychiatrist to overcome the frequent nightmares that would cause her to wake up screaming. It had also been good for her to get back to college where she was on her way toward obtaining a degree in Accounting.

As they approached the restaurant, Bobby's hand dropped down to feel Linda's belly. They both smiled. There was little discernable yet, but she was several months pregnant with their first child.

Bobby's father had been released from the state hospital again, only to suffer another relapse. He was now a patient at a private hospital specializing in the treatment of alcoholics. Bobby was hopeful that, with proper care and motivation he would be able to join them someday.

The neighborhood they were walking through seemed to be alive with the sounds of Latin music. It was like deja vous, especially when they walked into La Tasca to the strains of Tito Puente.

An elegantly dressed Cuban maitre di greeted them.

"Good evening. How many do you have in your party?"

"Buenos noches! Cinco. Prueba el postre; esta muy bueno," replied Bobby as he glanced at Linda for her reaction to his fluency.

"Very good, sir," replied the maitre de, chuckling to himself. "Please follow me."

"What's he laughing about?" Bobby asked, turning to Linda.

MAKI

"I think you got the first part right, but then you asked him to taste the dessert."

As they proceeded through the restaurant Bobby spied Carlos and his party at a corner table.

"Hold it, my good man. That's where we want to go," he said pointing to the table.

"Very good sir," replied the maitre de.

There was a very unusual center piece on the table. It wasn't at all decorative, and it was wrapped in cellophane and tied with a red ribbon.

"Oh my God," Bobby shouted, "This isn't what I think it is?"

"What the heck is it?" Alan asked, having never seen it.

"Well, it just happens to look like the knapsack I purchased at B.U. to put the money in. The same one I hid at the camp."

Carlos stood up smiling. "How are you, my good friend?" he asked as they embraced each other.

"That's really it, the famous money bag. Well, perhaps not as famous as the original briefcase, but it will do," said Bobby.

"In a place of honor," replied Carlos.

Bobby hadn't seen it since that terrible night at the camp when he had told Jim Heniger where it was. The knapsack and the money had been impounded by the FBI for several months, during which time all legal processes had been exhausted. In the final analysis, the statute of limitations had long run out, and since no one else had laid claim to the money, it had been returned to Bobby. Oh, the good state of Massachusetts had managed to usurp a sizable chunk of it for Capital Gains, but it had still left a significant amount of slightly moldy, but very spendable money.

Bobby had divided it between Carlos and himself. He then gave half of his share to Alan.

It was debatable if the money equated to the years of deprivation and fear, but it certainly had been enough to jump start the lives of all concerned.

Carlos introduced everyone to his father and mother, and sister Placida. Placida had become quite a celebrity in recent months in her new TV news anchor role.

Bobby did a double take when he saw who else was seated at the table next to Carlos.

"Do you remember this young lady?" Carlos asked looking at Linda.

Linda starred at the woman for several seconds before she recognized the FBI agent who was largely instrumental in getting her out of the car that night. Her face immediately lit up.

"Oh my gosh, Kerstin, wasn't it? I am so happy to see you again, because it will give me another opportunity to thank you. What in the world are you doing here?"

Everyone had a big hug for the brave young lady who had played such a large part in the successful culmination of the events at that camp, so many miles away.

"I had requested a reassignment shortly before working with Jim Heniger on your case, and I guess the commendation I received helped to hasten my re-assignment to this terrible place," she said smiling.

"They were cleaning out the old evidence locker back in Boston, and I thought the knapsack might be of some historical importance to you, so I brought it along."

"Well, we could always stuff it full of all the old memories we had, bring it down to the beach and bury it again," Bobby replied.

"Besides that," Kerstin said with a caring look toward Carlos, "I had to make sure that this dashing guy was behaving himself."

Bobby was pleased as he smiled at the handsome couple.

"You know . . . there's something been bugging me about that knapsack. That night when I was counting the money, I also discovered an envelope with some formulas and a small map."

"I know what you are going to ask," Kerstin replied quickly, "and all I can say is that the CIA was very happy to to receive that information. It was critical to our national defense, much more important than the money. It described a facility that they hadn't been able to precisely locate and the information in the envelope enabled them to get a fix on it."

"What kind of facility?" asked Alan.

"Well, it was a chemical facility, biological in nature."

"Biological ? As in germ warfare?" Bobby asked in amazement.

"Yes, I'm afraid so," Kerstin replied. "Once it was made known to Castro that we were aware of the exact location of the laboratory in the Sierra Meastra, several rounds of secret, back door diplomacy meetings were initiated. Ultimately, pressure was brought to bear on the Soviet Union and Cuba and they opted to disassemble the facility. I'm not privy to what that pressure might have been."

"Holy Havana!" replied Carlos looking at Bobby, "You mean we were involved in an international conspiracy and we did not even know it?"

"Yes, you were, Carlos. That man that killed Bronski and nearly killed you and Bobby was Victor Delazar from the so-called Cuban CIA. He was one of Castro's most entrusted operators. He was trained in the Soviet Union by the KGB and was actually considered to be the James Bond of Cuban intelligence.

Seems he had been somewhat of a rebel since birth, and had fallen in love and married a niece of the deposed dictator, Batista."

"Now that I think of it, I met this scoundrel a few times at some social functions with the Presidente," replied Carlos's father.

"Well, to make a long story short, he found himself becoming more sympathetic to the cause of his old school chum Fidel, in spite of being one of the favored few. He apparently had always the same discontent and desire for a free Cuba. Needless to say, his inside track to the Batista family had been very valuable to the rebel cause."

"A real snake in the grass," said Carlos looking at his parents who seemed transfixed by the story.

"He actually graduated from Wentworth Institutue six years before you guys got bounced and he remotely knew Carlos from the same social get-togethers that Mr. Almeida just alluded to.

He was a master at blending into the American culture. He could be very Boston or easily pass himself off as French Canadian, Polish, or even Russian because of his fluency with the languages and his expertise with disguises."

Everyone became silent for what seemed to be several minutes trying to digest the incredible information that Kerstin had entrusted them with.

The silence was broken, however, by the high pitched, yet strong voice of Christopher who had been listening politely. "Boy, am I hungry. When do we eat?"

Seriousness turned quickly to joy once again as Carlos's father shouted, "Everyone, please sit down. We must get to know all of you wonderful people better. Waiter, please see that everyone has a drink, and then we will eat. The masas de puerco is very good here!"

It was an extraordinary evening, one that would be repeated for years to come, and the happiness seemed more meaningful simply because everyone had experienced the depths of despair just months ago.

Carlos, Bobby and Alan sat side by side, and one could only imagine good things happening to them, and those who loved them.

Just as Bobby was to propose a toast, he glanced over at something Carlos had under the palm of his hand on the table, and Carlos replied, "Hey, Bobby, I have something here I want you to try. Come to the men's room with me."

Bobby was panic struck, and his face paled in remembrance of how it had all started almost a dozen years ago.

"You son of a Cuban ! This is where I came in!" he yelled.

No one but Carlos knew what the gesture had meant and he could hold his deadpan expression no longer as he turned his palm over to reveal a piece of napkin. They both gushed with laughter. Laughter that quickly infected the entire reunion party, causing the remaining patrons to wonder what the joviality could possibly mean.

EPILOG 2000

Four decades have passed since the tragic events at the Latino Club took place.

Bobby is sixty years old now. It took him five long years to become a practicing attorney in Miami. One of his first clients was Carlos's engineering firm. He has been specializing in defending the Cuban population of Florida. He is still very much in love with his work and his pretty wife, Linda. His Spanish has improved slightly.

Linda finally became a CPA, along with being a very busy mother to their two children, a boy and a girl. Both have already completed college and have good jobs.

Their son is engaged, and their daughter has been married for several years. She just made Linda and Bobby grandparents a few months ago.

Bobby's father was able to spend his remaining years in good health and communion with his family. He eventually passed away at the ripe old age of 92.

Alan had a very successful career on the PGA Tour, and when he became fifty he qualified for the Senior Tour where he continues to play. To the relief of many, he never did have to work in a Pro Shop again.

Judy continued to flourish in her musical career. Not to the extent of becoming famous, but enjoying what she was doing and sharing it with others. She eventually became a secondary school music teacher. She also sings professionally at weddings and local musical productions.

Christopher eventually went on to obtain a degree in Business Administration. He also caddied for Alan out on the tour for many years. He currently manages his father's affairs and has his own public relations business.

Judy and Alan were never able to have any more children.

Carlos . . . well, Carlos and Kerstin were a hot item for about a year until she was re-assigned to Los Angeles.

However, it didn't take long for Placida to fix him up with a charming young Cuban friend of hers. They were married in six months and now have four children, three boys and a girl. He continues to enjoy his work, and two of his sons have joined his company.

Placida is now a TV station manager in Tampa following an exciting career as a news anchor in front of the camera.

Carlos's father was stricken with a heart attack and died several years ago. His mother lives with him now. Except for some arthritis, she is in reasonably good health.

Carlos continues to foster and participate in activities that assist his fellow Cubans in getting to the United States.

The flicker of hope still remains for those hundreds of thousands of Cubans who would someday like to return to their native land. Many continue to risk their lives in all types of boats in their attempt to reach the United States and freedom.

President Fidel Castro continues his remarkably resilient and repressive control of his communist society, no longer embraced by the Soviet bear, nor by may other countries in the free world. His marathon speeches have diminished little and he still struts about in his familiar revolutionary olive drab. He will have the distinction of going down in history as the longest ruling communist dictator. A man of unwavering principals, if little else. A man who, to this day, continues to tear apart the Cuban people and his country's economy in the exercise of those dubious principals.

AKI

Fiction   Maki, Robert Nestor
MAKI   The briefcase.
(paper)
                        35112

FEB 15 01	DATE DUE		
MAR 29 01			
MAY 15 01			
JUN 06 01			

DISCARDED

BEALS MEMORIAL LIBRARY
50 Pleasant Street
Winchendon, Mass. 01475
tel. 297-0300